NATURAL
WONDERS

NATURAL
WONDERS

Angela Woodward

TUSCALOOSA

FC2 is an imprint of the University of Alabama Press

Inquiries about reproducing material from this work should be addressed to
the University of Alabama Press

Book Design: Publications Unit, Department of English, Illinois State
Univeristy, Director: Steve Halle, Production Assistant: Andrea Berns
Cover Design: Lou Robinson
Typeface: Garamond
⊗
The paper on which this book is printed meets the minimum requirements
of American National Standard for Information Sciences—Permanence of
Paper for Printed Library Materials, ANSI Z39.48–1984

Library of Congress Cataloging-in-Publication Data

Names: Woodward, Angela, 1962- author.
Title: Natural wonders / Angela Woodward ; foreword by Stacey Levine.
Description: Tuscaloosa, Alabama : FC2, 2016.
Identifiers: LCCN 2015041691 (print) | LCCN 2015049474 (ebook) |
ISBN
  9781573660556 (paperback) | ISBN 9781573668606 (E-book)
Subjects: LCSH: Widows--Fiction. | College teachers' spouses--Fiction. |
  Earth sciences--Fiction. | BISAC: FICTION / Literary.
Classification: LCC PS3623.O6825 N38 2016 (print) | LCC PS3623.O6825
(ebook)
  | DDC 813/.6--dc23
LC record available at http://lccn.loc.gov/2015041691

FOREWORD BY STACEY LEVINE

ANGELA WOODWARD'S *Natural Wonders* is a mesmerizing read. It starts with an old-fashioned slide show in a college lecture hall sometime during the twentieth century. The narrator is Jenny. Such a mild, near-antique-sounding name—the character describes it as made from "flimsy syllables." She is a young, near-faceless woman working in the college typing pool. While on the job, she meets Jonathan, a famous, late-middle-aged earth science professor who "specialize(s) in the human jaw," and who decides that Jenny is "sweet and good." When Jonathan precipitously suggests marriage, Jenny goes along with the haphazard idea. While observantly aware of the era's gender inequities, Jenny is obedient to outward appearances—and after Jonathan dies, she politely accommodates his faculty colleague, who requests that she tidy, edit, and organize her deceased husband's academic slide lectures.

The slide-lecture/treatise on the Earth's geological, paleontological, and anthropological history is *Natural Wonders'* narrative. Each chapter focuses on an aspect of that history and humanity's understanding of the earth, starting from the seventeenth century forward. Woodward's densely crafted anecdotes draw from accounts by European naturalists and anthropologists such as Milankovitch, Cuvier, Scheuchzer, Murchison, and others, who helped decode the wordless texts of glaciers, mountains' strata, volcanoes, and human and nonhuman fossils.

But any cursory summary will fail to represent this text's subtly amazing performance, and its textual innovations that come not from a desire to dismantle narrative or its form, but instead to burrow through it, shifting its weight and possible resonances curiously and to near-heartbreaking effect.

Like a miniature, eco-aware *Moby Dick*, this book travels the globe from Mongolia to Switzerland, Portugal to Greenland to Bermuda to Buenos Aires as the narrative pours with the dramatic, erotic story of life and the earth.

Hilariously, Jenny's lecture is aimed at a group of enervated student laggards doodling in their notebooks, who are unconvinced by the material, unable to be conscious of its vividness. Not only this, but the lecture has its troubles: There is off-topic drifting into fabulistic tangents. The technical assistant, Benji, seems to have disappeared, faultily loaded the slide carousel, or possibly has fallen asleep at the projector.

Woodward stays in amazing control of each wisp of her accrued motifs. Combined, the piled-on, yet intelligently controlled compendium of Earth history planked by delicious, sometimes dangerously strong folkloric tales, and even the cinematic glimpses of Jenny and Jonathan's thumbnail-sized courtship and marriage fill the novel's frame to the bursting point. Its sentences are amazingly modeled, belonging nowhere but to this half-glowing, built real-and-fictional creation where "a dark-loving hydrangea petiolaris chisels its delicate suckers," "the abundance of minerals from sea creatures hangs in tight lattices," and a shaman's bells are "voices of the unliving or of the mineral world."

There are other enjoyments. In flowing from one set piece to another, Woodward innovates with her extremely slight, vegetal scene shifts that are both abrupt and soft, the way sunlight changes through a window. Also, Jenny and Jonathan's short, tired marriage, set against the wider narrative on the world's humanless geologic epochs, creates a strange, anxiety-producing effect of suspension.

Natural Wonders is an amazing work about sentience and biologic magic, its structure built and layered with beautiful rigor. It is full of delicious sentences that will pull readers into its meditation on story-making and the awe that seems to be just outside our sight. Woodward's novel contextualizes our shred of a civilization so vividly that readers will see the world with new eyes. I am sure you will love it!

NATURAL
WONDERS

ICE AGES

BENJY, FIRST SLIDE, PLEASE.

Let me tell you about the age of the earth, he said. The English scientists worked together diligently and announced that the earth had been created on October 26, 4004 B.C. at nine in the morning. Out of formless mud, the sun rose and spread its light, the animals got to their feet and began wandering around the fields. Trees arched up, leaves unfolded out of thin twigs and cast shadows on the meadow irises, purple flags wavering under the nostrils of curious gazelles. Adam took Eve by the hand, he said, and twined her long hair around his arm. She laughed back at him, pressing her breasts against his bare skin. When they walked about, they never encountered their footprints in the damp ground—the earth was spongy and unmarkable, so new and fresh that it couldn't be stained or torn.

Everyone understood, he said, that this perfect state had soon been corrupted. But it provided a kind of balm, to look back on that splendid morning, especially in this, the late afternoon of civilization, where mugs of cider have left rings on the side table, the dogs have chewed the bottoms of the parlor doors, where every stroll through the town is adorned by drunks pissing against walls. Hardly a work of God was not knocked around a bit, fear making the animals fierce, smoke from charcoal graying the blue heavens. In so little time, the pure and bountiful earth had degraded, like a hard chopping block a butcher sets up in his new shop, a year later so scored and scratched, so percolated with blood and bile, that it stinks even at night when the shop is closed.

Several hundred years later, the Swiss doctor Agassiz made an extensive study of fossilized fish. He had spent the summer in Brazil, looking at a new cache. His colleagues plumped into folding chairs in the Neuchatel municipal hall, ready to hear more of his absorbing stories about his undersea monsters. Instead he talked about the glaciers in their native land. He blamed these sheets of ice for atrocious deformation of the earth. They had dragged with them rocks and debris, which now lay strewn in long, slovenly piles along the path of their retreat. The ice, shoving down into the rock, had alternately contracted and expanded, working its way miles down, disrupting the smooth layers and forcing up coarse material. Trickles of water had frozen into gigantic wedges, bursting solid mountains into canyon walls, now tracked and grooved. The great weight of the sheets of ice had shoved the earth's crust down and compacted it. Uneven folds of discarded soil built up into hills, while valleys showed where the ice had lain, like the hollow in a worn-out mattress. Deep oceans had filled places that were now desert, as the ice had put the land off balance. He had been showing them for the past four years his fish bones laid in stone, that he had brought back from the unlikeliest mountaintops. The whole of their beautiful Switzerland, he said, had been like Greenland, blighted with ice. The glaciers were reckless wastrels, now banished to the tops of the Alps, but they had had their way with Europe, gnashing and roiling it. There is hardly a place you can visit in our fair land, he said, where you don't see evidence of this frigid desecration.

They would much rather have seen his fine pencil drawings of fish scales. He rendered his creatures accurately but still gracefully, almost playfully, the long-ago flip-flop of the fish brought out in the panache of his lines. "Look around you," he said, describing plains scored into desolate polygons by the action of frost, rocks shattered into fragile flakes where once they had been coherent. This rough treatment had gone on for 12,000, perhaps 30,000 years. They felt sorry for the earth, much more than they already had, that it had been tormented down to its very core. Now everywhere they looked they saw traces of the ice's cruel tongue.

It was not so easy to convince the English. When Agassiz visited there the next year, he showed his colleagues a raw hillside, polished by the glacier's scour. But the Englishmen explained that for many years, small boys had been sliding down the hill. The rock was smooth owing to the press of their canvas backsides. The Swiss saw deep pockets where the ice had scooped out soft soil. He pointed out the sculpted shorelines of vanished lakes. All could be adequately explained by Noah's flood, they said. The English wondered why Agassiz was so insistent, whether he was not happy, not balanced. The Swiss was deepening and lengthening the sadness of the world, subjecting it to abuse it did not deserve. How had the land lain there and let itself be mauled by these sheets of ice? Why had it doubled over and buckled and cracked open under this superior force?

Next slide, Benjy, he said. Bring the lights a little lower. No, no. Use the dimmer. A little more. A little more please. That's it. Thank you, Benjy. Let's go on.

SMALL, BITTER VICTORY

BUT HERE JONATHAN'S NOTES are not so coherent. He's spilled coffee on them, or the cat vomited on them, a sheaf stuck together with sandy goo. It's not easy to be his editor. I would rather not have the task. I know nothing about his subject, but am simply his widow, the much younger woman Jonathan married seemingly to spite all those who said he wouldn't be so foolish. Jonathan died suddenly and unfussily, leaving everything to me to take care of. The will had scarcely settled in its safety deposit box before the lawyer drew it out again and began riffling through his cabinet for accompanying documents for me to sign. When Jonathan's department chair suggested I put together a memorial edition of his lectures, I wondered for a moment if he had confused me with Jonathan's first wife, Barbara. She could have done a good job. She knew his work, had helped him write some of his early papers, before she took their children and deserted him. "You understood him so well," Professor Williams said. That was hardly true. I saw him in a way none of his colleagues could have, but I doubt that's an advantage in this type of project.

Jonathan's introductory course on the earth and its prehistory started with the ice ages. It surprised him how little his students already knew, how they seemed to take the world around them at face value. Their understanding was right on par with that of the stout populace first faced with the earth's violent and tumultuous past. "Right, Jenny?" he said. I nodded, because it was always easier to agree with him, though I never knew when he was teasing me. My knowledge of students came from my time in the typing pool, where they had sometimes asked me for a pencil in order to scratch a note to some absent lord of their destiny. Like me, they would have agreed with anything he said, including that the earth was a large hollow ball with a garden in its core.

It seems to me Jonathan wanted to explain that time expanded and contracted, wheeling in and out, cast from the fisherman's rod into the turbulence, drawn back for inspection—ah, the hook's empty again. First God created the world in a twinkling, not that long ago. His creatures limped along, brutes really, until recently, dopes, children. Then the Swiss, the French, the Americans, even the English, measured the slow majesty of glacial progress and calculated back, adding thousands, millions of years to the world's age. Not that it would last any million years longer going forward. Cataclysm could smash all tonight. We still have only a moment to live.

"You're so soothing," Jonathan said to me the first time we went out alone together, when he, in all his nervous stiffness, asked me to have dinner with him at Puff's. I hardly knew him, had only spoken to him a few times, this rapid, disdainful man so much older than me. I almost thought he was asking me to eat with him out of misguided duty, as if taking me out was some obligation no one else had thought to attend to. He was likely gaining a small, bitter victory over his colleagues, showing them up for their thoughtlessness by showing some interest in me, which meant he really had no interest in me. The meal ground on, him entertaining me with tales of his travels, a brief mention of the absent children, now in college or beyond, and his hopes for another dig before he died. I scarcely had a life history by comparison, and found myself cast in the role of nodding and asking encouraging questions. I sputtered out, and he too held quiet, our awkwardness crumbling and fissuring the dainty white tabletop between us. "What a sweet, good nature you have," he said at last, in another voice entirely than the one that had narrated his discovery of a crushed skull in an ancient cliff.

ASTRONOMICAL THEORY

JONATHAN DIED RIGHT INSIDE the door, probably clutching at the coat hooks in the hallway before sliding to the linoleum. It was not at all what I expected, but no one else seemed exactly surprised. A man his age, taking up with a woman almost thirty years younger, had been asking for such a fate, they implied. His death was thus in a way my fault. "In the hallway, in the morning, right after I'd left for work," I found myself saying to his academic friends, to the one neighbor who knew his name after their many years on the same block, to my sister and mother on the phone. "In bed, then, naked," they answered, though no one said this aloud. They imagined a fatal passion between us, when in fact we had endured a short and disastrous dismay. We were both of us foolish, him for falling in love with me, me for not putting him off for his own good, his colleagues seemed to beam at me from their creased, reddened eyes. His department chair was the worst of these saddened stumblers, he who had actually okayed my time sheets when I had worked in the department as a temporary typist.

This one came over last night to encourage me. "So you're all right?" Professor Williams asked, standing in the hall, his feet right where Jonathan's silent head had lain. I told him I was much better, bearing up, doing as well as could be expected. There was no way I could tell him anything else. I had been alone before, and was alone again. He thought he was keeping me busy, keeping me from thinking about things, stopping me from "dwelling on the past," as he put it, by asking me to firm up my late hus-band's lectures on the earth and its prehistory. It's possible he saw this as a joke, a pun, I'm not sure. Jonathan and I hadn't had much history, just a quick, impulsive marriage, and a journey into geologic time would not make up for it. I made the professor coffee after he managed to follow me into the kitchen, apologiz-ing for the intrusion even though he had called first to make the appointment, then called again to confirm. I could see that by the time the water boiled and the brew dripped through the filter, we'd have nothing left to say. "The garden looks nice," he said, looking out at the one flowering something emerging from a bed of mud and bare sprouts. Jonathan had kept the garden. I was too ignorant to know which were the weeds, so now I did noth-ing to take care of it. All the fall stalks had collapsed in brown spirals. Jonathan would have managed to chop everything down to neat nubs, but I would have cut all the wrong things.

Professor Williams promised me that there was some money in it from the university press, if I would get on with the edition of Jonathan's lectures. Always hard to say if the press would be in funds, but apparently some biography had sold well, and a tome on the local furniture industry had found buyers. He encouraged me to get the thing finished. "Jonathan was always pretty orga-nized, wasn't he?" he asked me, as we nudged back down the hall to the front door. Jonathan's study gaped open, papers bundled on the desk, the floor, on top of the book shelf. Some of the books had their spines turned in and waved many multi-colored paper tags, set down under parts of the text he considered sig-nificant. The room struck me as a raft adrift, half sinking. Some-where near the center of the desk his black binder lay. Filled with Jonathan's finely schooled cursive and interspersed with letters and reviews, coverless decaying paperbacks, his magnum opus on jaw measurement, graded quizzes and paid heating bills, the thing offered me the barest inspiration for the history of the earth and its explorers. The job of collating the lectures seemed to be far more than puzzling out dates and acronyms, and yet in it I had already deciphered a bit more of his introductory course. "Good girl!" Professor Williams exclaimed, patting my arm. I had the idea he couldn't remember my first name, though he'd called me Jenny on the phone. He had always found me, during my brief employment under him, to be a conscientious typist.

So, to tell you more of what you need to know, Jonathan would have proceeded from the podium if we are to continue this dubious project, the earth seemed to have succumbed to the wicked depredations of the ice not once but perhaps four or seven times. The evidence piled up from every continent—thin double layers of sediment left behind in Swiss glacial lakes, a whole forest submerged and petrified just off Bermuda, acres of salt stretched across Utah, all that was left of a turbulent sea. Its creatures lay exposed as if still gasping for water, so plentiful that the geologists gathered them by flinging their hats blindfolded, then digging wherever they landed.

The whole system, they learned, from oceans to atmosphere, was powered by that fucker, the sun. And he was unstable, prone to spots and surges, throwing his radiation unevenly across the worried, wobbly planet. The poor earth's orbit had gone from stately zero, the fixture around which all else turned, to a lovely ellipse, to an irregular path that underwent "constant and significant change." It slumped, tilting somewhat, then straightened up as a stern word recalled it to its alert posture. The sun's radiation pinged it heavily and unevenly. The earth could hardly plan for this whimsical bombardment, and found itself flinching now this way now that, so that winters in one hemisphere lengthened, lasted far too long, catapulting us into an unhealthy spiral of cold. The earth skulked off, gradually stretching the time it spent roaming in the field. But when the sun whistled, it came limping back. So the blame lay on the sun, fickle, cruel—he was the one who caused the debilitating encroachment and retreat of the ice.

Only a master mathematician could hope to account for all the variables. At last the Serbian Milankovitch did the calculations, a precise measurement of solar radiation, first from his prison cell, then from Budapest. From his formulae he extruded 600,000 years of past climate data in stately mathematical rigidity. Not only his brother-in-law Wegener agreed with his conclusions, but all the European scientists read his manifesto, attended his lectures. His astronomical theory rose up complete and unassailable. They wrote him letters, not so much of capitulation but of gratitude for the steadiness of his hand. His dense pages of graphs, his eyes behind his gold glasses, led them to assign as incontrovertible his contention that he could determine the exact amount of the sun's heat that had reached the earth at any time in its long history. The ice ages fell along his graph, as well as the milder intervening tropical eras. Milankovitch also described with mathematical rigor the climates of Venus and Mars. He may have wondered about Saturn too, as he dug up weeds from the garden plot at the back of his townhouse. No place eluded the probe of his computations. And the physical evidence confirmed it. The strata found to be a certain age matched his charts—tropical flora for what he calculated were warm interglacials, the stony husks of ice oxen in layers he predicted had been laid down during an ice age.

Milankovitch devoted himself to his memoirs once he had published his solar radiation work. On the sunny west wall of his garden he grew an enormous Lady Banks rose. The yellow blooms climbed up the high enclosing wall and massed against the back alley of the bakery, reaching at last the baker's family's second story windows. On the east wall, a dark-loving hydrangea petiolaris chiseled its delicate suckers. After a few years of sporadic progress, the vine tripled in size. Its cool white sprays lit the morning, while Lady Banks blazed from eleven o'clock on. In such conditions, Milankovitch hardly felt the need to do more mathematics. When a few anomalies began to challenge his theory, he remarked that he didn't have the patience to indulge the ignorant with elementary explanations of his science.

Many wonders surfaced that same year. A biologist at Princeton found a map in an old mariner's guide in the basement of the library. It was a 17th century copy of a 14th century chart, which showed in precise detail the coastline of the continent of Antarctica—not the coastline at present, shrouded with ice, but the coastline as it might have been some 7,000 years ago, when the land itself had lain bare. He speculated that an advanced civilization had navigated the entire globe, long before the age of the pharaohs. Their maps may have been preserved in just a few places, most likely in the burned down library of Alexandria.

A French schoolgirl published a diary of a year-long sexual experiment she had finally broken free of. She had seduced an older man, who told her he admired the stretch of flesh between the hem of her outgrown skirt and her blue knee socks. At first it was all picnics and mattresses, but later he took her to cafes where he sat her in the laps of lesbian whores. One afternoon she allowed him to take her into the back room of a luggage shop, with two other men she didn't know. The three of them licked and kissed and fondled her 'til she was almost delirious, then they arranged her over a worktable so two of them could screw her while she sucked off the third. She wrote meticulously of vomiting out the spume afterwards, and the agony of her bowel movement the next day, so racking that her mother took her to the hospital. Behind the curtain, the doctor was shocked, solicitous, then he spat on her, telling her she was a disgrace to her family.

Soon after, she decided to hang herself. She took a clothesline back to the apple tree behind the house. Just as she was about to place the noose over her head, a gigantic black crow feather drifted down from the sky. She realized she was meant to write her story, to prevent other schoolgirls from making her same mistakes. And now grown men hold her book in their hands, so much wiser and steadier than they may have been if they had not turned its purely educational pages.

In England, the geologists took a sample that would have, by Milankovitch's reckoning, been 22,000 years old. But embedded in it was a bit of Roman brick. Some Germans decided to reexamine the Alpine river terraces that had seemed to conform exactly to Milankovitch's historical climate progression. It was clear to the new team that some warm water mollusks had been missed or misclassified. This essential data was now in dispute. Several years later, a band of English students probed what should have been an undisturbed layer of glaciated soil from 25,000 years earlier. At first they were elated, but later they turned up a rusted bicycle bell. Milankovitch was unperturbed. It would all come right eventually. He stood by his calculations.

Benjy, next slide please. No, not that way. Forward. Good boy. Thank you. Let's move on.

HOMO DILUVII

ALL RIGHT, BENJY, keep alert up there. Here we have, Jonathan would certainly have said next, Homo diluvii, unearthed by the Zuricher Dr. Scheuchzer, at Oeningen. This fossil, almost complete, had lain embedded in a silted shelf not far from the farm where his wife was raised. It surprised Scheuchzer that no one before him had come across evidence of early humans—that the skeletal imprints and paw marks, the impressions left in clay, were of hideous animals or gentle fern fronds. The men and women that God had wiped away in the Flood had vanished in their entirety until Scheuchzer stumbled across this strange, twisted thing. He dug it out whole and encased it in glass. The poor drowned creature shared modern man's outlines, with a few key differences. Scheuchzer knocked his pointer against the glass to draw his audience's eyes to the strange curvature of the spine. This stemmed from its general wickedness, Scheuchzer maintained, like hunchbacked old ladies, witches, goblins, this spinal deformity even now associated with terror and sin. Yet in his letter to the Royal Society, Scheuchzer noted that the sad remains had belonged to a man of exactly his own height, that is, "fifty-eight and a half Paris inches."

Scheuchzer seems to have been untroubled by Homo diluvii's strange, helmet-like head, crushed into two uneven plates. The flatness of its digits and its pronounced tail too he incorporated into his analysis of the slightly debased construction of the race of men God had eradicated.

"It's really a kind of thinking I want to get across," Jonathan told me, referring to his students, whom he considered an all too common type of sub-human, that is, undergraduates. The content of his lectures was secondary, especially as he had lost whole sections of it, left behind on the men's room radiator, and gotten it hopelessly interleaved with chapters of others' books he was reviewing, letters from his father, and his copious notes for other projects, his work on jaw measurement, the chatty memoir, never completed, of the dig he did with his first wife, Barbara. Jonathan and I married after knowing each other less than two months. While the judge recited the marriage decree, Jonathan dug his fingers into my waist, promising me an unalterable period of stability and affection. Yet I find over and over again in his lecture notes that the entire geophysical story has been one of *plasticity and change.* It's possible he didn't really believe this, or he put it aside for my sake, confident that here at last was something lasting. It seems nevertheless that Jonathan's tale of Scheuchzer's sinful skeleton is to be followed by the French anatomist Cuvier's discovery that the thing was not a man of any era, but a giant salamander.

This morning I reached for my coffee cup on its hook over the sink, and at the lip of the drain curled an enormous centipede. It didn't move as the shadow of my wrist flashed over it. Like all pests, it radiated a patient petulance, as if summoned by me and now slightly annoyed that I was late for our appointment. It had heaved itself up out of the plumbing for my benefit, or else let itself down the steep stainless steel slope. It had thrust itself through tiny cracks in the moist wood behind the drain board, waved its hundred pointed red legs free of confinement, in order to make this meeting time.

"Leave me alone," I told it. The sound of my voice didn't alert it to scurry away. It stayed in its spot below me, still expecting. All I had to do was turn on the faucet and the thing would be swept down the drain. But I didn't see why I needed to be the one to murder it. "Go away!" I said. I slapped the edge of the sink, making a warning vibration. All its legs rose up in order and resettled, like the oars of a longboat. This graceful motion brought it a little farther around the drain opening, but still in place for the water to hit it. It waited pensively for me to take action. We did not understand each other, unless it had showed up for exactly what it got, its final lesson, its meager consciousness extinguished in the blast from the tap.

This I can tell you, or have Jonathan intone for you: Cuvier was the only one with the knowledge of anatomy sufficient to overturn Scheuchzer's conclusions. As a poor student, Cuvier roamed the countryside collecting objects, which he drew obsessively back at the dimly lit table in his rooming house, rocks, rotten fence posts, leaves, buttons, polishing his vision by transforming it into precise gray lines. He early advanced to fill the post of Permanent Secretary of the Academy of Sciences, where he kept six standing desks all manned with assistants trained never to interrupt him. He wrote furiously across the creamy blankness of the open folio, then moved on to his next desk, where a different manuscript lay interrupted. He spent all morning rotating around the room, leaving off precisely at the bottom of the page, though this left the sentence, thought or paragraph abruptly curtailed. "Like a man entering a charnel house, I see on every side of me proofs of dead organisms," Cuvier inked in his precise hand. The multiple threads of natural development, he wrote, the orderly integration of families and species, had been brutally snapped time and again by a spiteful Nature. The world of the past, he wrote, was unimaginably different from our enlightened present. His vision of history was so sharpened that the blood still steamed on the floor. He spent much of his time drawing the musculature of the cat, the vocal organism of the canary. Every Sunday, he and his good friend walked the outskirts of Paris, finding all around the cafes and cathedrals the silt of an earlier world. They ground the alien and hostile past under their boots. Scheuchzer's man of Noah's time, now permanently interred in a museum in Haarlem, had dragged its belly along the ground. The sinful hands that had counted stolen money and groped helpless servant girls, Cuvier showed had been flippers tapering into sticky pads.

Jonathan and I had been reasonably comfortable together, and then not. One morning as I left for work, he leaned in to kiss my cheek, and I swerved sideways. As we both righted ourselves, our cheeks passed by each other, only a few inches apart, so that my refused intimacy nevertheless took me through the field of his heat, the smell of his scalp and shaving cream. A few months earlier, I might have inhaled with something like pleasure, or at least with nostalgia for the early moments of our love affair. I hadn't noticed the point at which his touch passed from pleasing me to irritating me, and now within the same tight orbit I seemed to have decided to evade contact altogether.

If Jonathan's notes were not here so blurred, I might be able to have him describe the expression on Scheuchzer's face when he looked at the lordly Cuvier's emphatic diagram of the salamander's limb structure. Most likely Scheuchzer would have refused to give over, in public at least. It was a man, he continued to claim, Homo diluvii, our reckless ancestor. He found many who believed him. In private, the scientist must have stared numbly at his fossil, the same gray trace in the rock now telling an ineradicably different story than it had when he first unearthed it.

THE MODERN

IT'S IMPOSSIBLE FOR ME to straighten all this out. Professor Williams has no idea of my difficulties. Jonathan spoke with such certainty, "The evidence is at last so strong that other explanations must now be discarded or modified." The only firm rule, he said, was that all the old junk has to go. It had taken what Jonathan broadly called the scientific community 120 years to agree that there had been an ice age, several of them. Now they fought on about what had caused these ancient debacles, and whether a sudden plunge into yet another era of unendurable cold could be predicted or prevented. All they discovered, he said, was that the world was in inexhaustible creeping flux. Rather than the reassuring progression of the seasons, even the magnetic pole of the earth had upended in a single tumultuous crush.

"What a sweet, good nature you have," he said to me at that first dinner. I wasn't going to disagree. He found me soothing, and I believed he was kind. He had introduced himself by shaking my hand, taken me out to eat, and later bought me a cup of coffee from the vending machine down the hall from my office. This scanty courtship had been evidence enough for both of us, at that point, that we were meant to live together in an easy, balmy companionship. It seems to me his own scholarship should have shown him that the kindest era gives way to a frozen solidity, or dangerous heat. When the evidence before us is at last incontrovertible, we must wipe away our earlier convictions, Jonathan's notes explain.

Milankovitch died unafraid, yet as soon as he was in the grave, his astronomical theory was declared void. It hung from the hand of a hotel maid, a rag full of holes, now used only to wipe the dust off the tables of the modern men of radio carbon dating. Milankovitch, a mathematician, had drawn a dazzling scenario with his calculations, but the scientists of two decades later now had the tooth-cracking inflexibility of physical facts. The fine equipment in post-war labs filled headphones with exuberant clicks and pings. This metallic chatter fixed the dates of fossil death, on the side of the living, this number; on the side of the deceased, this number. Therefore, all the gross, crude estimates of the 1930s had to be scrutinized anew. Fine cores drilled up from the sea bed showed millions of compressed skeletons of tiny foraminifera, first the warm water sects, then the cold water ones, who in life never met, had sworn enmity, inhabited different seas, did not send thin airmail envelopes between their separate families. The vivid graphs, red bars alternating with green, traced an entirely different trajectory of past climatic shifts than Milankovitch's stern calculations.

It was not possible that both sets of data could be correct. Milankovitch's astronomical theory and the now definitively dated fossil record were in direct conflict. A new theory was necessary. Though there was no doubt which would win, the modern and the older mode had to be pitted against each other. The confrontation took place at a conference in Rome, where the geologists hammered out once and for all an agreement as to the causes of the earth's unsettling fluctuations. After days of rain, the sun shone, and the scientists and their wives rushed out to see the sights. While they tossed coins into the Trevi fountain, an American tourist unaffiliated with the meeting plugged her curlers into the obliging foreign socket. Within a few minutes, the hotel's entire wiring system shorted out. The cooks stalked into the garden to smoke, but the maids went on changing the sheets in the dark. The manager had locked their working papers in his safe, and they were afraid to abandon their stations.

In Ballroom A, a German delivered his paper in French, to a lone American who understood a portion of it. Nevertheless, these two were in accord, and wrote out a pact: if the new time-lines were correct, then the ice itself had caused the ice ages, its own groaning weight ever reducing the temperature at which it melted, so that at the bottom, where the pressure was fiercest, the glaciers began to slip. On rollers of self-created melt wa-ter, the mountain ice sheets surged into the lowlands, cooling the oceans and bringing more ice. The sun had little to do with it. Change was sudden, apocalyptic, and capricious. A series of two or three harsh winters were demonstrably enough to tip the equation towards increasing cold. The ice as source of its own generation rang true to the scientists' hardy self-reliance.

The American woman stumbled down to the darkened ho-tel lobby. "Nothing works in this place!" she fumed to the desk clerk. "Power will be restored shortly," the clerk assured her. Just then, the grimy electricians burst in, toolboxes in hand, cigarettes dangling from their lips. The scientists straggled in from their afternoon outing, and seeing the confusion, left again for the corner bars. The woman began to weep, huddled in her new windbreaker. "This whole trip I haven't been able to do my hair," she sobbed. She was sure she looked awful.

Benjy, he said, move on please. Thank you. This is the mod-ern, he said: a cell, a safe, a locked box. Nothing gets in or out, no dust, no panting man, no woman stripping off her tights. The hands of clocks winding round and round seem so foolish next to the simple slide of lights from digit to digit. The old gas stations with their flip card numbers, crank rotating as father fills the tank, relinquish their place to blips of red flowing effortlessly one to the next. Content with this seamlessness, this uncluttered elegance, we can only shudder at the heavy-handedness of our ancestors, stuck in their dim analog innocence. The scientists of the 1960s now realized that the ice had built up on itself, and moved itself, and launched itself into the sea, until the formula tipped the other way, the earth snapped to her senses and said, "Enough!" The scientists agreeing on it instantly made it so. It had to have happened that way. The long undulations of warm to cold to warm had self-generated, the same way self-respect came from within, a man hanging his hat on a hook in his own hallway, rather than handing it to a pouty hat-check girl.

I'll bring his students into the auditorium to grumble and question. They jot down the formula for pressure and heat, inexactly copied from the dusty chalkboard. "What made the glaciers do what?" they complained. Those who recognized the formula from their physics class sat smugly quiet, but most of them had been assured that for this entry-level class, no chemistry or calculus would be required. Earth and Prehistory was suitable for poets and harpists, and attracted as well the lazy and the hungover. In the darkened hall, the students can hardly make out Jonathan's chalked lines anyway. They have not been provided a textbook to follow, only a dense, gray course pack full of disparate type sizes. I should be the one giving them something more coherent, which the press will publish in its memorial edition, a brief introduction from Professor Williams setting off my dutifully transcribed rendition of Jonathan's manuscript.

"Self-reliance," hisses the girl in the middle of the central row, who always seems to know what she's doing. She shows her notebook to the girls to her left, and they correct the symbols and numbers they had miscopied from the board. The ice's weight caused its cascade into the sea, where the resulting decline in water temperature locked everything down into an immovable ball.

"I doubt it," the students complain. No matter how much Jonathan has spouted off, they see no evidence of an ice age anywhere. They write down the formula because they have to, but they don't believe any of it. This one is too simple, anyway. "Since water under a glacier acts as a lubricant," they might have heard him say, but they've already put their pens down.

They scratch their legs, bare below the knee in their shorts and skirts. Their backs are wet, sweated to the prickly velvet seats. The sultry air of the old, unairconditioned hall seems much more convincing than the man behind the lectern, glaring down his nose into the darkness at their feet.

VEGETARIANISM

HERE ARE SOME WAYS to kill moles, mice, and rats. First, take a living mole, put her in an earthen pot, and stop the pot closed. Make a fire in the place where the moles gather, and put the pot on the fire. Immediately all the moles will gather to the pot on hearing the mole in the pot cry, and you may then kill them all. Similarly, take two or three living rats or mice and stop them up in a clay pot. Put the pot on the fire. All the rats and mice in the house, hearing the cry of those in the pot, will rush to the place, as if they intended by force to deliver their fellows out of the pot. Then you may kill them. Or here, take the head of a rat or mouse, pull the skin from it, and carry the head where the mice and rats usually come. They will immediately be gone from the place, running as if bewitched, and come no more.

This bit seems to have been copied out of an unlabeled book, a gray xerox bordered with the thready black of the back of the machine's cover. Perhaps it was the introduction to a lecture on hunting practices. I believe Jonathan knew quite a bit about that. He may have found it on the ground, or a woman in the Division of Domestic Sciences had given it to him, maybe at the start of their affair, maybe on its last day. There was no such woman, though. Despite their throwing themselves at him, after his wife's departure he had immured himself in his house for over fifteen years before he suddenly decided to take me to dinner at Puff's. I have no idea how this fragment of housekeeping advice found its way into his black binder. I should throw it out, or set it aside until its place becomes clear, but I'd rather leave it. I'm not qualified to put together Jonathan's lectures, but since I've been entrusted with the task, I'll do it in my own way.

What did ancient man eat? Jonathan's next lecture might begin. Probably that fits much further on. Jonathan specialized in the human jaw. By comparing the lengths and ratios of certain parts of them, he was able to reconstruct theoretically the larynx, softly decayed, and so decide whether the owner of a jaw, when alive, had been able to speak, or only to grunt and sigh. His magnum opus bellied out with charts, not set in the appendix but sprung right in the midst of the text, the existence of this marked with a one, the nonexistence of that marked with a zero, on and on across three pages, the type failingly small, the footnotes even smaller.

What ancient man ate, Jonathan said, concerns us. Listen, he said. After years of battling to overthrow his king and replace him with a more rational system, a hatmaker, Roger Crab, came home to London. But he quickly closed down his hat shop. His wife and two daughters had died while he was away, and the clangor of the streets hurt his ears. He found a remote spot on the coast and retired to a solitary life, where he survived on turnip greens boiled with wild oats. He drank only water, no spirits, and shunned meat of every type, even the insensate fish. This was such an unheard of way to live a life that visitors came to laugh and marvel at Crab. It didn't seem possible that a human being could survive on so little. Barons came to break bread with him, and journalists hung around the bushes, sure that Crab secretly ate veal at midnight. They posted a drawing of him in London windows showing his hips pressed up against a sheep's hindquarters, his arms tenderly circling its neck. This was the reason he ate no meat, they wrote. He loves it too much. Crab came to London to speak to a men's group, assorted would-be Levellers and Diggers, all the anti-monarchical political groups who agitated about their freedom and dignity, the order of society. Look, said Crab, flexing his arms, I am strong as any one of you, eating only the acorns that fall from the trees, raspberries and wild parsnip. All we need is right here. The earth provides.

Do you believe me? Jonathan said. Believe me, I am reading this to you out of a book.

The more dutiful students sift through the syllabus, looking for the proper week. Theories of ... *indecipherable*, they find. One or two raise their hands, but Jonathan can't see them in dark, or pretends not to notice them. Ahem, he says, let's go on.

Many years earlier, a Portuguese sea captain had blown off course and wrecked on the Indian coast. You remember this from last semester, don't you Benjy? Good. As the ship listed and stuck fast, the men staggered through hip-deep water onto the beach. They brought with them the image of their protectress, the Virgin Mary, nursing from her gold, spherical breast the holy infant. A tribe of wild, matted-haired men came to their assistance. Babbling their nonsense language, the savages made it clear that they would do no harm. They lit a bonfire of driftwood and seaweed to warm the stricken foreigners. The smell of the smoke was like nothing the Europeans had smelled before, though they had beaches of their own, and some of them had traveled the world over already, touching in at Florida, Cuba, Italy, and unnamed islands and peninsulas north and south. Thankful to have their lives, the sailors bowed down before their patroness and chanted their prayers. To their astonishment, the wild men too folded onto their knees and murmured the Latin with them. On this isolated stretch of coast the white men had not charted, the natives worshipped Christ.

The captain, nursing an injured shoulder, made signs to the tribesmen that he was the boss and should meet their boss. He touched the center of his forehead, indicating his rank. The tribesmen's brown torsos rose clean and muscular out of their white loin cloths. Under their hair, which grew like sponges or cauliflower, their foreheads radiated calm dignity. The captain exclaimed to his men how quickly the savages understood him. It was almost as if language was not necessary. These spiritual beings grasped with a look and a nod what the civilized sailors could only laboriously get across to each other with cloying strings of words. A remarkable people.

The captain bowed to the Banian king and spoke to him in Latin. To his disappointment, the king could not respond in the same tongue. Nevertheless, he made the foreigners welcome. They sat at a long table, but without chairs, and ate fruit and grain and sticky porridge. No meat at all graced the table. Afterwards, all the sailors and officers followed their hosts into a pillared building which enclosed a fire pit. The king waved to the priest to light the fire, and the whole company sank to their knees in worship.

The captain questioned the savages closely, though their power to answer was not what he had first hoped. He wanted to know how old the king was. The captain was the only educated man on the voyage, so he alone suspected the ship had run aground in the kingdom of Prester John. Prester John, a Christian not of Christendom, was said to be 200 years old. The pure, vegetarian diet of the Banians perhaps accounted for this lengthy life. How many summers had the king seen, he asked the savages. But since the coast basked in endless summer, they couldn't answer. Maybe, the captain thought, the king was immortal. Yet he noticed that when the king picked at a hangnail, it bled.

He composed a letter to his own king, though of course there was no way of getting it off. "The Christian piety of these people astounds me," he wrote. "They are filled with natural grace. They don't crush their lice, but pluck them off carefully and put them on a man whose special job is to give them his blood. They set out a sweet powder to feed the ants. If they find any insects in the house, they scoop them up and set them down safely outdoors. I have heard that the grave of Adam lies in this land, on top of a nearby mountain. We are getting up an expedition to go visit it. I hope to present to you both the bones of Adam and the living presence of Prester John, no myth, but a real man, even now playing in the next room with his two little daughters."

The captain was happiest when he planned. The present seemed to hang from his arms, or throb with the pain of his injured shoulder. The future though, like the open sea, gleamed with possibility. They set off inland, with eight of the Banians to guide them. They needed no mule or other pack animal. Sweet orange fruits filled their mouths whenever they needed a snack, and in the evenings, women appeared, though their villages were not apparent, bringing rice or their other puddingy grains. Rain cleaned them. They drank dew out of long, cup-shaped leaves. The afternoon sun warmed them, but not too much. The forest didn't even throw out thorns to rip their clothing. At last they reached a white marble sarcophagus on top of the mountain. Here Adam rested. The outlines of the original Eden could still be seen, the sculpted paths now overgrown with moss and vines, but with the earlier pattern sticking through. A gang of holy men kept up the area, and worshipped every morning for five hours. The captain surmised that they had lived on here uninterrupted by the Flood. A page may have at some time fallen out of the Bible, he thought.

A few key verses could have explained how these men came to be here, when the rest of humanity had perished.

Towards the end of the afternoon, a cow wandered into the holy grounds. The Portuguese got up and shooed it, gesturing with the backs of their hands. The cow stared at them uncomprehendingly. It wouldn't budge. It lowered its head and began chewing the grass of the Garden of Eden. A couple of the men went up to it and swatted it. Sailors, they hadn't seen cows for half their lives, but they remembered them well. The cow moved on a bit, but they couldn't get it to leave.

It was only later, back on the coast with their ship mostly refitted, that the Portuguese understood that their hosts worshipped cows. A couple of them had learned the native language pretty well, but even without words, they gathered from the way the animals wandered through the Banian territory that cows were holy and not to be harmed. These Christians who had knelt to Jesus and Mary clung to a disgusting heresy. The captain tried to persuade Prester John that worshipping cows was idolatry. Didn't he know the story of the golden calf? But the king was completely ignorant of Bible stories. Holy mother and infant he understood, but Christ the man he was confused by. A painting of a blue-skinned devil hung in the little temple. Isn't this Christ, said the king? Krishna?

The sailors caught prawns in the surf and roasted them. Homesick for meat, they also trapped and cooked a kind of water rat. The Banians' glutinous porridge gave them gas, and many of them spent their afternoons doubled over, holding their bellies. Long starry evenings they devoted to talking about sausage. Work on the ship always stretched on one more day, one more week. They longed to be gone. They would head straight home. But the wood they used for the repairs didn't dry right, and the major patching had to be torn out and started from the beginning again. Bored and sick, they started taunting the Banians. They went into the woods and dug up worms. Then they ran to the center of the settlement and threatened to crush the worms to death. At once a flock of men and women vied to ransom the worms. In this way, the men collected mounds of beautifully carved coconut buttons.

Back in Portugal, the sailors promised each other to say nothing of their encounter in India. They felt sickened by the memory of praying in the heathen temple, which they had mistaken for the church of God. It couldn't have been Adam buried in the crypt on the mountain, but some trivial ancestor of the Banians. Maybe it was even a cow or a serpent in the tomb. The shave-haired priests had filled the sailors' ears with their chanting, infecting their brains. They spent their wages in the port bars. They intended to give their women the coconut buttons, but they didn't want to tell the story of how they came by them. They could still feel the worms wriggling in their palms, and see their protectors running off with them to place them safely in shady soil. The sailors felt entirely degraded by their contact with the vegetarians, and plowed into tripe and blood sausage and calf brains with gusto. But meat didn't taste the same. It had about it the possibility of not eating it, its negative, like a ghost on the stairs. Regret was its horrible aftertaste.

INTERPRETATION

ALL DOWN THE HALL, from behind the partially opened doors shaded with pebbled glass and decorated with gaunt black letters spelling out names of inhabitants most likely long vanished, the clacking of typewriters rang out. At certain hours, the students rushed through the first floor, flooding into or out of the auditorium, but on the floors above, only a few footsteps disturbed the ancient radiator heat. A burnt coffee smell from the vending machine mixed with the odor of the dust that lay in deep strips along the tops of the filing cabinets. The filing cabinet drawers sometimes heaved out, wheezing metallically, and then slammed in with a definite, grateful percussion. The tapping of the typewriters braided through the occasional clanking of the janitor and his cart, the whistle of the restroom door at the end of the hall and the mutterings of its plumbing. The ringing of a phone was stilled immediately by a high-pitched voice, and then by a series of low assents. It wasn't clear who could have cared what the typists were typing, as long as the sound continued, the hum of the gears, the harsh, happy ping of the rotating wheel returning to center, the coughing of the paper being wound into or out of the clasping rollers.

When I became one of its citizens, I added my own forceful tapping to the chorus up and down the hall. The professors blasted by me, sometimes nodding hello, sometimes asking my name for the second or third time and still not getting it right. Jonathan was the only one who had slowed, and forced his bulging briefcase under his opposite elbow so he could put out his hand to me in a manly and formal gesture.

"Good morning," Jonathan said. "Excuse me for a being a few minutes late. Not as late as several of you," he observed, as the doors in the rear of the auditorium swung open and then closed with their pompous, deliberate tonk behind the backs of the tardy.

Why is he late, the students whispered? He's never late. Must have stayed in bed with his new wife. New wife? Him? Yes. Remember. She came in that one day, and sat right in the middle. Thirty years younger than him. Didn't you hear?

But I can't imagine the students cared anything for Jonathan's personal life. He was for them a kind of automaton that they activated by their pressure on the seats. Once enough rears had sunk into the old, worn velvet, the thing on stage began fiddling with his glasses, flipping through his notes, and gesturing to the boy in the projection booth. Next slide, Benjy. The students could all imitate him. "No, not that one. Forward, let's go on," they said, adding gravel to their voices, sniffing, and looking down. But we won't let the students get away with their own lecture. Who knows what they'd want to talk about, sex, surely, those vulvas painted on the walls of the caves in France. It took the archaeologists years to puzzle out a single bounding antelope, but the vulval slits showed themselves unequivocally, a few simple lines indicating nothing less than that source of pleasure and generation, of mystic union.

Interpretation, Jonathan said, is vigorously condemned by many of my colleagues. We don't interpret, they say, he said. We only note the facts, and draw from them limited and reasonable conclusions. Interpretation implies fancifulness, and scientists are not fanciful, my colleagues claim. We are in no sense creative.

Our theories are founded on the best available facts, and if theories often change, that is because new facts have been unearthed. You should see, Jonathan said, the letters section of *Geophysical Annals*, where the scientists throw barbs at each other, and then pull them out of each other's flesh, each delicate imputation causing wounds at both entrance and exit.

The students have concluded this is to be the long-promised lecture on hunting practices, how standing upright to throw a spear stimulated the development of brain matter, and the calculus needed to plot the trajectory of a projectile in motion spurred the growth of our sprawling concrete civilization. They thumb through their gray course notes until they find a smudged sheet filled with formulas and graphs. A few students squint down at them, while others groan and flip pages, looking for something a little bit more comprehensible.

This Jonathan won't give them, his notes here as usual a wreck of deletions, three pages titled "Interpretation" upside down but nicely hole-punched anyway, as if he had intended them to go in reversed, like a tarot card promising not the overflow of fortune but fortune's draining away. Ahem, Jonathan said. Excuse me for this morning's late start. Please turn to chapter *incomprehensible* and look at the paragraph under the heading *indecipherable*. All good? Benjy? Thank you. The pursuit of mountain climbing belongs to our fairly recent history, he said. The need to claim the very top as a nationalistic fetish dates to an era less than an eye blink behind us in geologic time. The peaks were consigned to dragons and ice ogres, local maps quite legibly spelling out the names of these creatures' caves. And though the alpine villagers might never have seen these fantastical creatures, they had heard them, and swore up and down to any surveyor or prospector that irrefutable evidence convinced them of the impassibility of the higher slopes. Our friend Agassiz, if you can remember back to our first lecture, camped out in a high meadow, digging up from beneath the plants peculiar to this elevation strange stones crimped into the shapes of nautilus and sea sponge. In the evenings he lit a lantern in his goatskin tent and pored over these strange formations. Their ridges and indentations cast dark shadows on themselves, keener in the lamplight than in the dull midday sun. He cleaned them with a series of brushes, taking out first a big stiff scrubber, then down to finer and softer boar, and then camel hair. In the dark he ran his fingers over the graduated bumps, so exactly like the hinged covering of the crayfish tail that he could not believe it was not exactly that, a crustacean made of stone. All during his months of quiet excavation, his ears filled with a ting-ting-ting raining down from above. He thought at first it was tinnitus, a disarrangement of his ear. It rang out softly in the background, now here, now there. "What's that sound?" he asked the goat herder, when he passed through. The boy told him it was Claudius in his workshop, a gigantic immortal silversmith who lived up the slope. Agassiz wasn't sure the boy was serious. But soon he found he was, that they all believed a giant squatted in a sheltered overhang and rapped at metal with his hammers. "And what does he make?" Agassiz asked in the village bar, when he had gone down for supplies one afternoon. "The most beautiful things," the girl told him. She ran off, then came back in a swirl of skirt, wiping her hands on her apron. She had with her a tiny seashell, brushed with silver on its edges. She tilted her palm so Agassiz could see the light gleaming off it. "Where did you get this?" he asked her. She smiled and unhooked the guard on the back. As she leaned in to him, he understood he was to pin it on her blouse. His hands, so adept with pencil, brush, shovel, and pick, lost their confidence with her white cotton. He fumbled with it, pushing the pin end fruitlessly into the little holder. As he breathed in, the barmaid breathed in too, and her breasts came towards him, then sank away. He had thought she was no more than sixteen, but looking closer at her cheeks, he realized she must be almost his own age, twenty-eight, perhaps quite set in her ways. He straightened up, the brooch now winking at him. It was hardly the work of an immortal. A shore-dwelling visitor must have given her this touristy trinket. The silver paint had flaked off in places, and the clasp was a little loose, held on with cheap glue.

"I'm staying up in the meadow," he said to her. "As you know."

"As I know," she answered. The door yawned open and slammed behind her as a group of farmers came in. Agassiz thought he had never seen such unprepossessing people as these mountain folk, one-eyed, hunched, limping, twisted, though many of the young women had wonderful complexions.

What flinty bargainers they were too, so that Agassiz couldn't make any progress in his negotiations for rope and tallow. He ended up taking a room above the bar. Even though it was summer, the light wouldn't last long enough for him to get back up to his camp. He put his boots outside the door and lay listening to voices in the corridor. He imagined the knob turning of its own, and then the shush of her bare feet along the boards. He dropped off, and woke later to a tapping sound. Why doesn't she just come in, he wondered? But the sound came from another direction. The door lay still, the knob unhandled. The rhythmic knock-knock-knock slowed, paused, then took up again. That giant, he thought, at work even at night. He saw a squid waving its tentacles at him, strange outsize eyes staring at him from the anvil. The giant pounded, and the sea creature elongated, becoming thinner and pearlescent. Its narrow tentacle at last reached all the way to Agassiz's cheek. Just as it was about to make contact, he awoke again with a start. The knocking came louder and faster, and was accompanied now by a single cry, "Wait!" The room, the corridor, the building, even the night sky outside the window lay taut and still in the wake of this one outburst.

Fifty years later, an amply supplied crew hiked up past Agassiz's meadow and surveyed the brink of the glacier. It thrust its fingers down at them, little icy channels, and in places revealed rivulets made entirely of stones. The stones clacked against each other in a continuous chatter. From within the depths of the glacier came pops and bangs, sometimes going off right under the cleated boots of the mountain climbers. At the top, other peaks looked down at the climbers, harsh in the unshielded sunlight. "What is that noise?" one of them said on their way down. "It's never stopped the whole time we've been up here." His companions hadn't even noticed. They were preoccupied with the tightness or looseness of the knots of their equipment, and their own perilous progress, the descent much more dangerous than the glorious upcoming.

"How was it?" asked the sister of one of the climbers, when he was back safely to their uncle's farm. She had stayed there all summer, as had been their habit after their parents died. The rest of the time, they'd both been away at school. The climber brought back no photographs, the process being too cumbersome in this era, but Benjy, thank you, here. He told her what he could. "The gravel lay in a streambed, exactly like water, but all made of tiny rocks," he told her. "That night, we were delayed for hours when Paul lost his knife. It seemed only a few minutes we were looking, but before we knew it, it had gotten completely dark. We'd set down our packs, and we couldn't find the one that had the lantern in it. It must have been right next to us, but we couldn't find it again. We had to set off with no light. It was deadly cold, and started to snow."

"But it was July," his sister said. He'd written her the whole story in a letter, and told it at the dinner table too. This version was just for her.

"It can happen. It was late July, anyway." The August heat still kept them captive on the farm, languorous mugginess sending the vegetables into ecstasy. He noticed that his sister wasn't listening. He only wanted to tell her the last part, how they were saved. She went to the window and drew the curtain aside. A yellow rectangle from one of the outbuildings twinkled across the dark yard. One of his uncle's hired men must be still putting away tools. The climber explained how they had found their way by the supernatural light of the river of stones. Some force higher up had set the whole cascade moving downstream, the stones gamboling over each other and catching sparks. Rock in a perfect imitation of water now became fire. As the current moved, the struck sparks seemed to race downstream, the bright flares leading them on.

His sister turned from the window with a smile. Her expression didn't at all fit the story he'd been telling her. Of course he'd told it before, but not just to her. He wondered about it later, tucked under the cold sheets his aunt had ironed smooth. Down below, a soft, rapid tap of footsteps followed a sigh of hinge. He looked under the curtain of the window just over his bed. A black outline drew itself across the yard, a squiggled shape incoherent in the shadows. After that, he couldn't sleep. He went down the hallway to retrieve his book. He stopped at his sister's door and knocked quietly. She didn't answer. "Sally," he whispered. He turned the knob, but found no one within. How strange, he thought. She too must have forgotten something. She might have been washing something she needed to wear tomorrow, down in the sink in the kitchen.

All down the hall, from behind the partially opened doors shaded with pebbled glass decorated with gaunt black letters spelling out names of inhabitants most likely long vanished, the clacking of typewriters rang out. On my first tentative day at this temporary assignment, the noise had seemed incessant. "What are they all doing?" I asked the woman who sat senior to me at the further desk. She looked up briefly from her own machine. The browning tendrils of an overgrown spider plant divided the space between us. I had been given very little to do, though I had been promised a long list of textbooks would need to be made up soon. The air hung heavy with dust, not only from the tops of the hulking file cabinets but from the mineral samples and fossils that had accumulated on top of and alongside many dirty display cases. "They told me you type 72 words a minute," she said. I had gotten through the department memos and the meeting minutes already, and no other tasks were on offer. She said nothing else, but implied that I was free to do whatever I wanted with my time, since I was so quick with my work. I took a break and walked down the hall, where a dry terrarium occupied a windowsill. The sounds of the typewriters continued, as if the work of the college were being advanced furiously, without pause. This was only the most obvious interpretation. The typists invisible behind their shaded doors may have been writing any kind of material, novels, romances, editorials, petitions, their children's reports on jaguars or jaguarundi, instruction manuals, prayers, letters to their sisters.

THE SCALE OF IT ALL

AFTER OUR INITIAL CLINCHING together, Jonathan and I cooled off quite a bit. One morning as I left for work, he leaned in to kiss my cheek, and I swerved sideways. As we both righted ourselves, our cheeks passed by each other, only a few inches apart, so that my refused intimacy nevertheless took me through the field of his heat, the smell of his scalp and shaving cream. A few months earlier, I might have inhaled with something like pleasure, or at least with nostalgia for the early moments of our love affair. Now it was a relief to be just outside his orbit.

Let me explain geologic time, he said to the darkened lecture hall. The scale of it all takes some imagination to comprehend.

The students put down their pencils. Imagination is not their job.

What if, he said, you were reading a story. The story concerns a man bitten by a mosquito. He walks to the back of the yard to dead-head the daylilies. Possibly he wishes his wife would do it, seeing as she has so much more time than he has, but then again, she doesn't seem to know much about flowers. If he left the task to her, she might cut off the buds before they bloom. He thinks about the cloud passing over, wondering if it will rain tomorrow, and every few feet he stops to pull a weed. The front of the garden is in sun, but falls into shade at a certain point, and there the bugs swarm. The new flowers hold their yellow faces towards him, open, happy, while yesterday's flowers have drawn in to gaunt sleeves. If the withered fringes are removed, the flowers bloom again, so he moves towards them with purpose, his fingers ready to pinch them off. As he reaches towards the first flower, a mosquito lands on his arm. He swats it.

The man's life goes on for forty more years. He has a baby, he rises through the ranks at the construction company where he sorts the bids and contracts, he buys a summer house, he becomes a mellower, wiser man than in his youth, he takes the grandkids fishing.

The mosquito, however, has in the course of one day had her beginning and met her end. She crawled out of her larval sac that morning, flew around the yard, and met a handsome devil who made love to her. After their sortie, her lover disappeared, and she was left pregnant, starving, wild with desire for mammal blood. "If only that one will hold still," she thinks. She slips her stinger into the man's pore, then plunges her poison in to release the flow. Darkness descends, no, not this time, let me live, let my children live!

Her whole life has passed in eight hours. Buried in the bottom of the exclamation point at the end of her story is another story, in type so small you cannot read it. This story perhaps concerns a volcano. Once it rose from the equator, but over 80 million years, forces beneath it squeezed and shifted it all the way to the pole, where it joined a chain of fiery fellows, and gradually flickered out.

Inside the last full stop in this story written inside the exclamation point of the preceding one lies another story, in even more minuscule type. This one is about dust sprinkling outward after an explosion so loud it wiped out the hearing and memory of the dust, which was once a whole something, and is now fragmented. Over an uncountable stretch of time, during which the dust fell, revolved, flowed aimlessly away from its origin, it cohered with more dust, circled and backed into yet more, until the dust formed an uneven clot. The clot compressed and cooled until it became recognizably a sphere, that is, it would have looked like a sphere from far away, from the vantage point of a gigantic, distant sentient being. But in fact no consciousness, and no one, was around to read the tiny writing that told its story. Inside the last period of the story of the earth coiled another story, so dense that its ink drop held the mass of a billion galaxies. This dot was so heavy that it sliced through all matter, like a hair falling off a sweater, unnoticed, abandoned, the universe let loose into ever vaster, slower emptiness.

That first evening when he took me to Puff's, Jonathan told me later, he had already determined to marry me. Not sure what to say to me, he was distracted with worry about where he had stored his insurance and retirement papers, which he'd have to amend with a new beneficiary. When we stood to leave, he came around behind as if to pull out my chair. I had already stood, needed no help extricating myself from the tight, dark spot between tables. He lunged at the chair back anyway, shifting it as if punishing it, then half behind me, half beside, he collapsed all his weight into me, his face in my hair. The busboy squished by us with his plastic tub, the soiled rag waving over the end of it. I could just see, around the corner of Jonathan's suit jacket, another couple rising, the woman wiping her lipstick on the napkin and dropping it, the man squinting at the bill and laying money on the waiter's little lacquered tray.

Jonathan turned his face to me, revealing in its sad, slack openness an utter desolation. I stood paralyzed in its intense shimmer. "Well, now," he said in something like his normal voice, then turned away again to cough over his sleeve. I couldn't say anything, not even "there, there." I didn't have the strength to acknowledge what I'd seen, even though after he brought his face back to its typical composed outwardness, I could see he knew I'd recognized his longing. I coughed a bit myself, and thanked him for the meal. He looked at me again and cleared his throat. That was all. We parted awkwardly outside the restaurant, standing too far apart to touch, the streetlight in our eyes. I imagined that was the end of it, that we wouldn't be able to speak to each other again.

COSMOGENESIS

THE STUDENTS LOOKED DOWN at their notebooks, where their hands seemed to have scrawled, "a mysterious mimetic force drifted down from the stars." Some of them crossed it out. It didn't sound very scientific. But most of the others left it there, because it didn't matter to them: if Jonathan had said it, they would transcribe it, and later attempt to memorize what might appear on the midterm. Jonathan and I married in the City-County Building scarcely two months after our first meeting, when he swept into the department office and spied an unfamiliar woman sitting behind the massive typewriter. He had juggled his books and papers and cup of coffee into his other arm so that he could put out his right hand for me to shake, though such a manly and formal gesture seemed to me totally unnecessary. Where all the rest of them had blasted past me, sometimes calling "good morning!" sometimes asking my name for a second or third time and still not getting it, Jonathan had slowed down, squeezing his coffee cup into his elbow, and introduced himself.

"Who is that?" I asked the other secretary, when he'd gone on. "Oh, him," she said. "His wife left him, took the kids and moved to Arizona fifteen years ago." It seemed that that explained everything about him, or all I would need to know. That he taught Earth and Prehistory and was an expert on jaw measurement lay outside my requirements. My intersection with him would be fleshly and material, nothing to do with his mental and spiritual preoccupations, or with mine.

The students have the formula for phosphorus and manganese in their notes, but they've missed his explanation of the mysterious *materia pinguis*. Again it was the Swiss, and some of their French and Italian neighbors, who couldn't help but stumble over fish bones, seashells, whorled nautilus, high on the mountains where they could not have been washed by any sea. Sometimes these figured stones lay in piles, layer upon layer, as if a whole abandoned beach had been thrown up under the goat pasture. The most convincing explanation for these odd replicas of marine animals was that a mysterious plastic force under the earth produced them in coincidental mimicry. Jack Frost painted the windows with meadow flowers, and these were inorganic, in no way derived from vegetable life. In the same way, the *materia pinguis* concreted under the earth, shark's teeth, scallop fans, created by this underground petrifying juice.

Not quite right, demurred the Italians. The juice did not derive from the earth, but rather, the mimetic force was beamed down into the earth from the stars. These devious flickering lights were capable of infiltrating the soil and coiling dumb minerals into spirals or spiny jaws. Anyone who had studied the nature of the stars by sitting out under them on a hillside at night would understand that they changed things. By their persistent twinkling, they shed the *materia pinguis*, and it seeped down onto buried fruits and leaves, conjuring them into stone creatures, these crabs and swordfish etched in rock.

Benjy, he said, I have the wrong notes in front of me. I'm sorry. Where were we?

The students sigh and rip that page out of their notebooks. The floor of the auditorium is suddenly littered with crumpled paper. They should have known that an argument about the nature of fossils was covered much earlier on. But the professor has been dreamy and distracted lately. One of them saw him sitting on a bench behind the lecture hall, talking to a woman. Actually, no, none of them would even recognize him outside of the auditorium. I swear it was him, the student says. They were talking. So what? He can talk. No, honestly, they were talking together, sitting close and kind of leaning in towards each other. I swear he has a girlfriend.

But this is not evidence enough for most of them, or not part of a compelling narrative. The man behind the lectern shuffles through his papers, while the students imagine themselves the boys that cleared the rocks from a cave entrance and let themselves down into it. Their bleary flashlights picked out the horses and bison running along the walls. In a pack, the boys hurry to report their find to Abbe Breuil. But now they're out of the story, and the good father continues his investigations of the great cave of Lascaux, and many others. Twenty years later, an artist called the Abbe from New York. He was painting a mural for the museum that was to show the cave artists in the midst of composition. Would they have spread their paint out on an elk scapula, like an artist's palette, he asked? Did they have oil lamps? Abbe Breuil answered yes to these. And what of those mysterious vulvas, the artist asked. Why are the walls of so many of the caves covered with sketches of the thighs of women, pubic triangles, the vulval slit, and so rarely an entire human figure? He'll include none of those in his painting. After all, children would see it. But he was interested in the Abbe's opinion.

I have no idea, answered Breuil. Perhaps they worshipped women for their generative powers.

Hanging up the phone, the Abbe walked out into the kitchen. The housekeeper had left coffee for him, warm on the back of the stove. He sat at the little table and looked down into the scratches in the wood. He saw a mammoth tooth in the wood grain, and slightly elongated, its twisting neck. A tiny gouge became its eye. When he moved his saucer, a series of nicks linked up into a reindeer swimming, chin thrust up to keep it out of the water. He thought of his sister spooning gruel into the baby's mouth while she called over her shoulder to her husband that he should wear his other suit. It was going to rain later, she said, and the light suit would get wrinkled. The heavier one would stand up better. Her husband didn't answer, but when he came back into the kitchen, he had changed his clothes.

The Abbe stared down through the table, into the world beneath. He had been raised with the belief that there were three interconnected worlds: one below, of base reasons and desires, one above, of pure heavenly love, and a world in between, where people spent their lives struggling to make decisions. He saw now below the table a different world, where a different, microcosmic Abbe sat. That one had chosen every different path from the Abbe he knew, and so was not an Abbe, had left school, loved women. This one's eyes hadn't squinted down into books, and so wore no little round glasses. He had run around outdoors more, and so grown taller. The way he sat in a chair was more relaxed, and also more temporary. He would get up soon, stretch his arms, and go outside and look at his car. "Mimi!" he called. "What?" came a foggy answer. A woman in a bathrobe wandered into the kitchen of the world below. Her hair lay in thick tangles, as if she'd just gotten out of bed. She began scratching around the stove, looking for the box of matches. "I'm going out," the anti-Abbe said to her back. "Coffee?" she said. The man grunted. She came up very close to him when she set the cup down and then lingered by his chair, her hip pressed into his side. Neither of them spoke again.

The Abbe looked away from the wood grain and the anti-world went back into its closet. He had begun a correspondence with the other most famous French archaeologist, who was also a man of faith. "The world of the past is so different from what we expected," he wrote. "Does this change what we believe about the future of mankind?"

Teilhard de Chardin wrote back, all the way from China where he had discovered Peking Man. Ultimately, he wrote, we will be reborn outside of time and space. We will crawl out of the earth and leave it behind us. Our planet will circulate through space, bleached white like a fossil, with no motion across its surface. At that point, we will have evolved into an ultimate synthesis with god's love. Looking at the transformations of the past, he wrote, it's clear that our world is headed towards a radical remaking I call *cosmogenesis*, where what was heavy and dense, particulate and individual, will become once again light and undifferentiated, a diffuse anti-matter made up entirely of god's affection.

What are we supposed to write down, the students wonder? Around their formulae they've scratched elaborate whorls, criss-crossed pen lines making a dense texture across the bland, blue-lined notebook paper. Patterns form, then disappear. They can't find the date of the midterm. He's already changed it twice. They put their hands up. Sir? He's taken his glasses off and stands at the front, his head bowed, looking at his knuckles. Excuse me. What out of all this are we supposed … sir? When is … sir? Are you all right?

Yes. Thank you so much for asking. Let's get on with it. Benjy, please.

LAKE VOSTOK

BENJY, NEXT SLIDE, PLEASE. Thank you.

Sir, sir?

No, this is what I want. He hasn't made a mistake. Thank you, Benjy. At least we know they're paying attention.

The projector's beam illuminated a cylinder of dust motes swimming up and down in the rank air of the auditorium, while a dense rectangle of black swallowed the screen.

Darkness, he said. What can we ever truly see or know? This will be on your exam. Please take good notes today, ha ha. All that we've discovered lay under the earth, where light does not penetrate. Abbe Breuil crept into the cave with a candle, which bravely shone until he got to the depths of the chamber where he found the paintings of mammoths, you remember from last week. In this wide gallery, the dripping walls stepped back from him. The candle flame began to falter. The Abbe suspected that an air shaft long blocked led to the surface, perhaps an earlier entrance that an avalanche had closed. As his light flickered, the animals began to move. They bobbed their heads and winked their eyes. They swung their trunks, and he wondered why he had told only an eleven-year-old boy where he was going. If the rocks shifted again and cut off his retreat, he would remain here under the earth, at the mercy of the painted animals.

It's all right, the Abbe told himself. The animals only existed as long as the flame burned. In the dark, they would return to invisibility. He, though unable to see himself, would continue to exist for a while because he had a mind and a spirit. Even after his death, his sister, carrying the blue pot of oxtail soup from kitchen to dining room, would see him in her mind, probably his younger self, the reckless, ambitious boy.

In our enlightened era, we use chemical analysis to detect the relic's hidden presence under the earth. Next slide, please. These carefully mapped core samples show here was their pile of excrement, here their pottery works. Next slide. These three surveys illustrate the full range of possible results—1) locating an expected skeleton 2) failing to locate any skeleton, and 3) locating an unexpected skeleton. Phosphorus forms long-lasting compounds with certain minerals, leaving a chemical residue of human activity. Yet for the earliest groups, who had no fixed settlement, soil analysis finds no trace. Next slide please, Benjy: a trough, dark dirt, and in the bottom someone seems to have sketched a rudimentary skeleton. Its legs knob up slightly at the knees and continue on into two loops, a kind of caricature pelvis. A crinkly spine and two wisps of arms connect to a childish, outlined head. Iron and manganese drew this awkward cartoon, he said. As microbes consumed the skeleton, they exchanged its calcium for their heavier elements. What was white became blackish brown, though no light lit the world inside the soil, so all in fact was colorless until exposed, he said. Where the skeleton had once rested, stretched out, chemical leaching had produced a stain. Hence when his colleague dug this one up, she found much less than a skeleton, only its vague impression.

He let it rest lightly, this "she" in what has overwhelmingly been the story of men and their adventures. Assuredly *she* was the wife of a colleague, and though fully qualified, entered the annals through his last name. They've been everywhere together, this husband-and-wife team, though we can imagine that he stepped up to the conductor with the tickets in his hand, even if it was she, with her fluent French, who purchased them. Dark men, too, and their even darker wives, remained bit players at best, as the Swiss, the Americans, even the Finns, swept to the poles, to the equator, to the mountaintops, and to desolate Greenland with their superior drills and ground-penetrating radar. Living people with all their complications had very little to do with the layered cores brought back to the lab and examined for the flip, flip, of oxygen isotopes that distinguished cold sea water from warm.

Though a new theory had been agreed upon at the conference in Rome, more evidence was essential. Accordingly, the advanced nations launched the International Geophysical Year, he said, in which much was to be discovered, determined, understood, and laid to rest. Interdisciplinary teams of scientists attacked both poles, looking for history in the ancient ice. Yet the year itself stretched on for eighteen months, an anomaly, for sure. Off Greenland, the waves chopped against the rowboat as the sailors lowered the heavy equipment off the Intrepid IV. Ice blown in on sea spray coated the winch almost six inches thick, and the box of drill bits swung at the end of the chain uneasily, the burden bashing the ship at one end and threatening the sailors' heads at the other end of the arc. When they cut through the ice with the blow torch, they nicked the winch's spine. Its sudden sag sent the equipment into the sea. The winch itself now seemed to stare into the water, head bent over the rail in the posture of a man unable to believe his bad luck.

The Americans on the other pole fared little better. At first, their exploit went well, and they dug down three thousand feet. The ice cores released from their fat pipe drill slept in a special built trench arched over with plywood. Crawling underneath with fluorescent lamps, they lit the light summer bands and the darker, dustier winter relics. But meltwater and gravel quickly clogged the machinery, the cook lacerated his hand, and the heavy seaplane, coming in to re-supply midseason, listed into a snowbank, tilting its cargo rupturously. Despite the tall tower that climbed aristocratically over the drill pit, the geophysicists felt themselves pushed back to grunting manual labor, hauling the ungrateful equipment on their backs, unclogging the snow machine treads with whisk brooms and boot brushes, nothing more sophisticated than Dickensian orphans might have handled. Their search for the earth's past led them a hundred years into their own.

The Soviets, camped over the ridge, got on quickly and in secrecy. They must have brought with them an imp dug up from a tsarist dungeon, who fitted one black tube into another and slotted them effortlessly into the ice cap. The waste water curled away from the devil's machine, whimpering sideways rather than plaguing them with residue. The comrades could be spied through binoculars walking always with purpose, even though bent over in the wind, carrying significant-looking canvas duffels. Though they had swift machines for riding over the snow and ice, the Soviets had brought dogs as well. The double lens of the binoculars showed the animals healthy and playful, burrowing into the snow and leaping out again, jaws snapping joyfully.

At a détente dinner the two camps agreed to eat a ham. The Soviets brought rutabaga, while the Americans poured boiled water over desiccated flakes to make reconstituted mashed potatoes. Puritans and atheists alike drank whiskey. Over the little glasses, they alluded to their progress, the Yanks showing their calluses and demonstrating pulled muscles, the Ivans remarking on how well they slept, the surprising ease of the operation. "Flawlessly," the chief officer intoned. They had already sunk almost two miles down, the ice so compressed at that depth that the air bubbles had collapsed into solid crystal. When the dense oxygen pellets thawed, the ancient gases unfurled into mirages of diamond palaces, floating blue and pink under the iron ceiling of the hut. These fantasies expired with a scent of jasmine and osmanthus, the intoxicating pollen of the Permo-Cambrian tropics. They had set the striated ice cores to music, the lighter bands pegged to treble notes, the darker to bass. The Soviet scientists conducted their calculations and analyses to this telluric opera. Most intriguing of all, the chief went on, they had detected just a few more meters down a giant lake, unfrozen water sloshing in the dark.

As the Americans didn't believe, the whole drunken party whooped up the dogs and sledged to where the Soviet spire glittered over the ice pit. The drill at rest shuddered lightly, still in tune with the softly pulsing cavern beneath it. Laying their ears to the wooden floor, they heard the distinct slap of waves, as if they were sunbathing on a dock. The chief officer passed around a map, which showed the hidden water bigger than Duck Lake, Green Lake, Lake Monona, any of the blue wonders the Americans had summered on. Yet this lake had an entirely different character, trapped beneath 200,000 years of polar accumulation. The sun had not warmed it for all that time, though the heat of the earth's center kept it fluid. It paced back and forth in its cage, a forgotten panther turning restlessly.

One of the geologists put on the record of the ice opera. After the initial pop and fizz of the needle, the high and low voices alternated, "haaa ... ho ... haaa ... ho," pitch aligned with the formula off the spectrometer. Still with their ears to the floor, the men took in the repetitive curling waves of Lake Vostok, an ostinato to the song of the ice that pealed out of the phonograph. The Soviets unscrewed the lightbulbs, leaving only the record player hooked to the generator. The generator's voice had gone on unnoticed, its pensive rumble underpinning the entire evening. In the dark, the red "on" light of the Victrola gained intensity. It created its own landscape of partial faces out of the features of the men sitting on either side of it.

Earlier, the geologists had discussed what undiscovered bacteria, what exceptional fossils, might be found in the black lake and the mud beneath it. All those wishing to understand the earth and its climate, past and future, would find key evidence by dredging the lake. It was possible that animals lived down there, not only shape-changing amoebas but blind salamanders and wraith-like colorless fish. Our planet's fertility continued to astound, that algae and diatoms might float through the sunless water, taking nourishment from some other source, from magnetism, from the water's sinuous currents.

Nevertheless, the will to discover seemed to have left the encampment. When the record spun to its last groove, the man nearest hopped up to reset the arm and start it over from the beginning. The lake whispering below suffered no interruption. It had been going on this way, locked beneath unseen, for their whole lives. Now, pinned below the imminent drill, the black water continued to knock against its containing walls, the alternating rustles wounding, healing, subsuming, regenerating. Though the cartographers had penned its outline on their charts, its restless motion swept on, regardless of anyone who would observe it.

THE ORIGIN OF LANGUAGE

JONATHAN EXPIRED IN OUR HALLWAY, having said nothing more to me as parting words than "I'll see you this evening." I saw him that night, but he did not see me, his glasses askew, face turned down, his body already stiff, and as cold as the unforgiving linoleum he rested on. When his department chair suggested that I put together a memorial to Jonathan's work at the college, a definitive edition of his lectures on the earth and its prehistory, I thought he must have confused me with Jonathan's first wife, Barbara. She in fact had helped write some of his early papers, before she took their children and decamped to Arizona. Despite my unpreparedness, I dug through Jonathan's black binder, strewn as it was with extraneous matter, clippings his father mailed him, detritus from an alumni magazine, pages of book reviews, and leftover student papers notated on the bottom "see me" or "insufficient," or in one case, "crude but good." Jonathan's magnum opus on jaw measurement obtruded itself many times over. I could make nothing of it, embellished as it was with a dense chart, the existence of this feature indicated by a one, the non-existence of this feature indicated by a zero. I am sure, though, that the origin of language must have been a part of his course, that he expected his students to note and speculate, not just on the earth, but on the small bands of proto-humans who roamed it with very little record beyond their smashed and petrified fragments of bone.

Could ancient man speak? I imagine at some point he would

have directed this question at the students in the lecture hall. Let us approach this scientifically, he advised. The French society of linguistics, he said, finally solved the problem of the origin of language in 1865. Written into its bylaws was the abolition of any study of this question. Members who raised inquiries as to who had been the first speakers, what was speech, whether Hebrew was the primordial language or was it some other, did sheep herders with their endless vocabulary of ewes, lambs, shearing, spinning, soft undercoat, long fiber, felt, fat, dogs, dye, invent speech by creating an industry that needed a technical vocabulary, or did primitive peoples find themselves imitating the calls of birds as communication across the plains during the hunt: such people were free to continue with these unsolvable imponderables, but only outside the hall of the academy, after they had surrendered their card of membership with all its explicit privileges and responsibilities. The members in good standing continued happily, he said, to track the changing shapes of vowels as they made their way across proto-Hattic to pre-Anatolian, and to designate uncertain scripts with variant A, variant B, variant C. Meanwhile the maids who made the cocoa for the little girls spoke with a halting lisp that they acquired on donning the apron. The children might chat with their servants all day without once sounding their S's in that servile manner. When the maids commanded the coachman to stop fooling around and get the horses ready *tout de suite*, they formed their consonants quite differently, while the lady of the house spoke ever softer and higher the more she worried about her approaching thirty-fifth birthday.

The French, Jonathan said, dammed the river for a time, but they were not able to quash for good these perverse speculations. Many scholars deduced back from Latin, from French, from Celtic, from Latvian, the original tongue as spoken by all the early people of the earth. Our living languages are dialects of this ancient speech, they claimed, and our decay away from its resonant syllables to our own sloppy pronunciation caused all our woes, from plagues and wars to the fact that young people when out walking in the woods tend to talk about their other friends who are not with them, and what clothes they wear, and how much money Robert lost at blackjack, rather than listening to the trees, which speak to them through the rustling of their leaves.

They had many methods for unearthing the lost original language. Benjy, slide please. Please pronounce these syllables with me: AG, BAG, DWAG, GWAG, LAG, MAG, NAG, RAG, and SWAG. These nine primordial speech blocks are the basis of all further words, according to a Scotchman who went on to produce three volumes of fine print explaining his methodology. AG, BAG, DWAG and GWAG all refer to hitting or striking. The other five imply different actions of physical force such as pressing, scraping, and dragging. Nothing further was needed by our ancestors, who were fixated on the actions of their hands.

Other toilers similarly worked backwards to find the original twenty-two nouns. Verbs they frowned upon as later folly. They derided adjectives, and would have burned them, choked them, stuffed them in a bag and drowned them by their thousands if they could have. How much have we lost, yet how much still remains to us, cried the linguists to each other in their journals—let us return to the few pure sounds, the H, the L, and the R. When the tongue moves back and the throat breathes out, we feel peace and openness. To pronounce N with the tip of the tongue in the front of the palate creates a spirit of sickliness, leading to all the diseases of negativity, when the first man created the words "no, not, never."

Cuvier was the only one with the anatomical skill to demonstrate that the orangutan was not capable of speech. And my own work, he said, which has focused, as you may know, on the human jaw, has added much to this debate about the earliest capacity for speech. Even crania we find crushed, flattened, broken and burnt have measurable specifics, which when compared with a wealth of other data realize ratios from which we can calculate the probable length and diameter of the larynx. From this we can begin to determine whether this creature or that creature was physically capable of speech, or merely of grunts and cries.

This is certain, wrote Jones: the letter O represents the first human sound. It means the infinite, as well as surprise, wonder, there you are! Fear, resignation, and the restoration of hope. This, Jones contended, was scientifically demonstrable, out of pure rational deduction. Today's sounds, he wrote, the words of modern mankind, and especially their alphabetic scripts, have devolved into random systems of meaning, a kind of mutually recognized and agreed-upon schema, whereas the sounds made by early man all referred directly to either the natural world or to the state of the soul. And why do we need so many words? All we need are words that communicate what one body feels, so that another body can also feel it. Justice, he said, has no location in the chest or the wrist. Abstraction of any kind is a desecration.

It won't surprise you, then, Jonathan said, that Jones recruited a group of experimental subjects to live in a small band in Lithuania speaking only the prescribed words that constituted the first language. He gave them all a vocabulary list with 216 words on it. They contracted to study and memorize the list, and then to live in the linguistic simplicity of its confines for an entire year. Their official words included otter, salmon, bee, honey, as well as danger, tiredness, love, sickness. Verbs were limited to pull, push, mash, and assorted other daily actions. Communion with the divine was to be done by the participants in silence, if they found it necessary to pray. "I've seen a salmon!" said a poor, crazed woman who had lost her child, to an out-of-work brick-layer. Jones had paid them half the fee in advance. If they stayed in the village and confined their speech to the list, he would pay the rest into bank accounts he had set up for their use in Vilnius at the end of the term. Her utterance sounded something like, "Ak gwale laksa!" Jones and his several closest correspondents had argued fiercely over the existence of a past tense in the ur-tongue. While no traces remained of a future tense, and all the other tenses seemed clearly to be bastardizations of a once-in-vincible present tense, a few remnant speech particles seemed to point to some kind of understanding of the past. The experi-ment was not perfect, but it was worth carrying out.

Jones circulated among his subjects once a week, noting their conversation as well as their actions. He had warned them that they would be fined for any infractions of their vocabulary, and those that informed on the others would be rewarded. The first few weeks saw many mistakes, as the experimental subjects had only had a little time to memorize the word list. A woman burst out with "God damn!" when hot soup spilled on her. "Shit!" would have been allowable, but she had to pay for invoking an artifice. Some boys from the nearby town hung on the fence, taunting. Unable to answer back, one of the subjects responded by shoving the smallest boy in the chest. He then could not ex-plain to the angered mother why he had attacked the child. Jones had to intercede.

But soon the assembled subjects had learned the primor-dial tongue fluently. They sat together in the evenings, repeat-ing the phrases they liked best. "Their whole manner and facial expression has softened," Jones wrote. "I would like to observe more closely the musculature of their cheeks, but even on casual observation one notices a kind of smooth radiance about their features. This comes, we may hypothesize, from the harmony of their words both with their natural surroundings and with their human natures."

As winter drew in, the experimental subjects spoke less and less. Rather than stringing their words together to tell back their activities, or to make requests—"Drag this here!"—they sighed, pointed, or huffed in exasperation. Quietness gave way to sullenness. The group had formed two cliques, with a small third party somewhat in between. This party was the most verbal, carrying words to and fro between the others. Eventually the two main groupings didn't speak to each other at all, and among their own kind, they seemed to understand each other so mutually and completely that no words were necessary. One evening, two men in the faction of taller, stronger individuals strangled with their bare hands two of the members of the in-between group. The remaining neutral parties escaped to the other camp. Now the experiment raged in silence, the small rural compound divided into two warring halves.

Jones was obliged to halt the experiment in the wake of the murders. He begged the participants to let him interview them, but most of them fled back to their ex-husbands, alleys, mental hospitals, public parks, and liquor stores. He was determined to wring as much data as he could out of the burst and rotten remains of the experience. His most significant publication speculated on the role of weaving in language development, noting the similar motion of the shuttle left and right between the strings of the loom and the significant verbal output of the go-betweens who had carried messages between the "strength" faction and the other group.

Jones had his heyday, especially when it could be shown that men had been the first weavers, and women had descended to the task only when it lost its allegorical presence and became the humdrum creation of blankets. But later experimental work eclipsed his: language had developed, said his detractors, on the open plain, in all cases in the presence of horses. Study after study bore this out, so that to be a Jonesian was to cling to an outmoded, laughable heresy, and not to go galloping over the veldt, the drumming of hooves corresponding perfectly to mankind's eternal internal pulse.

GONDWANALAND

JONATHAN HAS SOME BEAUTIFUL DRAWINGS of diatoms here, plus a terse note to me: *remember to take my black shoes in today*, as the day before and the day before that, I had forgotten to stop by the resoling shop for him. It's a wonder that he kept that, a mark of my rebellion and neglect, because I had stopped wanting to do those little favors for him long before he stopped wanting to do them for me. "What a sweet, good nature you have," he told me continually, as if this assertion could keep away the decay that had set in only months after our hasty wedding. After our initial clinching together, we cooled off quite a bit. One morning as I left for work, he leaned in to kiss my cheek, and I swerved sideways. As we both righted ourselves, our cheeks passed by each other, only a few inches apart, so that my refused intimacy nevertheless took me through the field of his heat, the smell of his scalp and shaving cream. Earlier, I might have inhaled with something like pleasure, or at least with nostalgia for the first moments of our love affair. Now it was a relief to be just outside his orbit.

Professor Williams gave me another call to see how I was getting on. "I type 72 words a minute," I told him. "Wonderful," he said. "Amazing." I let him imagine a neat white stack of corrasable bond growing at my elbow. In the depths of Jonathan's binder I found something about a train fire, the drivers getting down and playing cards by the tracks while the engine burst out wands of orange flame; pages of a review of something that began with praise and descended into scathing denunciation: "like a rope ladder with missing rungs, Preston's latest work sends the reader on a perilous journey towards an unlikely and unsatisfying destination," ending with conciliation—"the prose is sound though workmanlike"—and noting errors of punctuation, translation, and dates. One of his students, I assume, left him a scribble in a spiky, European-looking hand: "If you don't raise my grade by seven points, my government will not renew my scholarship, and I will be returned to my uncle's business, as I told you when I came to your office last week."

The entire geophysical story, Jonathan wrote elsewhere, amid other notations—Gas gauge broken?/Send card to Dad/ Ask Jeremy for *indecipherable*—has been one of plasticity and change, with endless probing, venturing and testing of ... *indecipherable*. Benjy, he said. You know the one I mean. Yes. Raise your hands, now, if you know what this is.

The students keep their hands in their laps, or cover their mouths with them, or doodle assiduously, not even glancing at the screen. He probably liked that best, their keeping quiet, stunned by mystery or simply uncomprehending. He shows them the putative singular continent Gondwana, all the earth's land focused over the unforgiving South Pole. The Sahara sprouted streams and lakes, while humid India offered snack shops and ski lifts, humble Alpine resorts, dry, cool, refreshing.

The paths of the glaciers, he said, in many instances showed ice flowing uphill, out of the sea and onto the land, a most unlikely configuration. Milankovitch's brother-in-law Wegener posited an explanation, that the continents had unpegged themselves from the turtles' backs they balanced on and roved across the oceans, at one point cramming together in a massive, single island. Under the groaning out-press of the ice, the land had stretched like taffy, then broke itself screaming into individual parts. The mountainous coasts are no more than heaps of scar tissue. What's more, the scars along South America can be matched to the weeping flesh along the edge of Africa, where they notch together exactly, a former unity now torn apart. Look a little closer, and she, South America, nestles her head on the shoulder of he, heroic Africa. They breathed thus together, no need to speak. 'I'll take care of you.' 'I know you will.' But now deep ocean separates them, and she fumes at him: 'He's gone down the street to live with that hussy, but he still has the nerve to drop his laundry off for me to do. Just wanted to see the kids, he says. Has he once asked me how I am?'

When Wegener was no more than fourteen, his mother's friend used to visit them at their summer place. Usually as soon as she came in the house, she made her way to his mother's room, where they sat behind the curtained doors, talking for hours. The high-pitched voices twittered through the afternoon like silver wire sawing through the boy's boredom. His father and brothers came up at the weekend and shot ducks, but most of the time he moped alone, the mildewed scent of the antique books another key ingredient to the overwhelming lassitude of the long vacation. One afternoon she, Julie, walked over through a terrific storm. His mother was in bed with a cold. "Julie, you can dry your things by the fire!" she called. "Have Alfie put the screen up." Wegener dragged the two Chinese screens together in front of the fireplace and beckoned his mother's friend, wondering as he did this why he was so biddable in this instance. When she asked him to pick up his socks or throw away the plum pits he'd left scattered all over the floor, he wouldn't do it. But he set the furniture right for Miss Beckman, who stepped behind. The prints of her wet bare feet glared from the dark floorboards. In a moment, a pair of arms emerged over the top of the screen, laying the dripping dress over. With a swishing sound, two white stockings slithered alongside the dress. Water fell from their toes, and a puddle spread at the base of the screen.

"Is the fire hot enough?" his mother called. "Are you drying off?"

"Brrrr ... I'll be fine in a minute," she said.

Wegener stood to go, slightly nauseous, gripping his book in his hand. But his mother called him to her room, to bring a bathrobe to her friend.

He took the thin plaid flannel, again wondering why he was being such a good boy. He should have cleared off.

"Miss Beckman," he said. "Here's something dry to put on."

Rather than reaching over the top, her hand appeared between the two screens. She had pushed them slightly apart. "Thank you, Alfred," she said, looking at him levelly through the little gap. Without lowering his eyes, he could see her breasts rounding up against the slinky material of her slip, the damp cloth clinging to her stomach and legs. She raised one arm and ran her fingers through her hair, lifting it away from her face. Then she turned away from him, and he scuttled off to his room upstairs.

Though Wegener had done much to publicize and laud Milankovitch's astronomical theory, his own theory of continental drift could not be rescued from ridicule. "One can see clearly," Wegener wrote in *Geophysical Annals,* "the way our present continents fit together like so many puzzle pieces." But though it was clear, his drawings mysteriously compelling, all it meant was that here was more debasement, fall from an initial unity, as the land masses swept unmoored, little more than fragile rafts on the tumultuous ocean.

"Poor Julie," his mother said later. "You know she was raped by soldiers during the war. She's terrified of men." Wegener continued to eat his bread. When his father came up, she might ignore her youngest, but with no one else to chatter to, he couldn't avoid her confidences.

He biked to Julie's house and knocked on the back gate. "Oh, it's you," she said, "and I was just napping." He followed her into the bedroom, where they rolled around, he fully clothed, she in a loose dress that unbuttoned itself. Her breasts and belly smashed against him, her roundness so in contrast to his thin, sharp neediness. "Your face," she said, laughing, "Relax." He had been set in a mask of fury, as if taking a math exam. She smoothed his eyebrows, releasing a pure, happy calm, a feeling almost unknown to him. Seeing him smile, she cried out, then wriggled higher so that her nipple found his mouth. The vastness of his pleasure was unimaginable, a quandary—if this could be, then how could the rest of life be endured?

THE ISLAND OF DOCTOR MONTGOMERY

WHEN I MOVED INTO JONATHAN'S HOUSE, unaltered since his first wife's time, I often couldn't sleep. I woke up in the middle of the night and lay for hours, exhausted but fully conscious. I wanted Jonathan to soothe me and shush me, and considered that part of his role. Most of the time, though, I couldn't wake him. Yet always he complained to me that thoughts flooded his brain, the most mundane things—he wasn't sure what weight twine to buy, we were running low on milk or coffee, a student complained about a grade. "He hasn't learned one thing! Nothing!" he said, but still the student settled into his office every other day to wheedle and plead. When these cares assaulted him, I was somehow sleeping deeply. He couldn't rouse me. He told me I mumbled things to him, "Don't worry, go back to sleep," words he considered generic, when he wanted my genuine comforting. I never remembered any of this. And so in some kind of pendulum motion, a perfect symmetry of insomnia separated us, one of us distraught, the other one peaceful.

On a rare night when he came to bed early and I hadn't dropped off yet, he told me about one of the Mongol tribes' funeral rites, or lack of them. Evil spirits instantly infected the dead—the moment the breath left the body, the devils set up camp, hammered nails into the walls to hang their ancestral paintings, rearranged the inner organs into a comfortable semi-circle and took up their hellish chanting. This belief necessitated the quick disposal of corpses. They loaded the departed onto on open cart and lashed the ponies. The body, not tied down or wedged with pillows, at the very most wrapped in felt to ease the heaving up onto the vehicle, at some point bounced out and fell behind the fleeing carriage. The driver was not to look back. He must do everything in his power not to notice the point at which the body fell. His fear was that it would jam against the sideboard, one leg, one arm dragging, the rest secure. He hallooed the horses into a mad zigzag over rocks and ruts. The dogs, loosed from their ropes, followed howling. They tore the cursed flesh to bits. The whole enterprise took about half an hour, he told me, from death to remnant.

However, I don't think that tale was part of his course. I found a stack of papers I hadn't noticed before, in the corner on the floor. The only thing legible on the first page, the rest smeared as if long underwater, read in Jonathan's fine Catholic school script, "Two years later, I am not in the same extreme state, but some of it still applies." As I stood staring at the blurred blue of the rest of it, I noticed a tiny pattering. Ant eggs, like half grains of rice, rolled off the bottom of the sheet of paper. On the floor below, tiny black figures scurried in all directions, the rescued children clamped in their jaws. I dropped the sheet I was holding, covering up the whole insect civilization that had somehow forged its territory inside the study. I was so shaken by my disgust at the little creatures that I sat in Jonathan's chair for an hour, hardly able to move. I had left a cup of coffee on the bookshelf, but I couldn't even reach over to get it. It seemed safer to stay exactly where I was.

Consequently, I've decided to put this chapter together from whatever's nearby, his children's books, or perhaps my own well-worn paperbacks that he was kind enough to give me shelf room for. It's not that there's nothing of mine in this room, though in fact there's very little. I should hand the whole project off to Professor Williams. He can have it. I've already told you about the shipwrecked Portuguese, Jonathan may have said as the lights in the auditorium came down. Benjy, no, we've seen that one. Thank you. Imagine a little wooden boat, encrusted with dirt, an evil bilgy smell rising from the coils of rope, only one oar left, and your companions, two dead men. At least you have their measures of water, but their hard tack has been swept away in an enormous wave that swamped the boat and let their torsos come bobbing up to your seat in the back. You can't throw them overboard. The three of you tied yourselves securely so you wouldn't be washed away, and you'll never get their knots undone in your weakened state. But forget it, none of you students could have endured this, watching the dead men's blank eyes watch you, while the waves tumbled gray on gray one after another, the horizon a blurry fog, no color, just the endless up and down motion of the disturbed sea. I don't put it to our undergraduates to survive that. Well, maybe Benjy could. Benjy's a special case. He could survive quite a lot. Good boy.

No, this was a poor Scottish medical student, Prenswick, sole survivor of the *Ventura* taking him to Buenos Aires. Miraculously, when the life boat broke up in the surf, he came away with only a concussion, and woke in a drafty cabin, dry land, sheets scratching his chin. The peace of the plank bed, which didn't buck up and down but lay flat and still, the emptiness of the chair facing him, absent his rotting companions, the cessation of the salt spray that had battered his skin for days, made him cry into his cupped hands. Later when he woke again, he was pleased to find that he was on an island occupied by a venerable London physician, a Dr. Montgomery, a kind and good man. The lonely island was supplied with its own fresh water spring, as well as with French wine, with coconut and breadfruit and tinned puddings and ham. They ate at a rickety table in the breezeway of the doctor's laboratory, the clatter of their knives and forks mixed with the howls of monkeys in the trees.

Possibly while all this was happening, Prenswick lost, his family out of their minds with worry, somewhere back home a sour-faced man visited a fortuneteller. He sat down at the glass table. The magician tapped his orb, and the tabletop resolved into a window showing the world outside in thirty years. The man, who had inherited a cutlery shop and eventually became the biggest landlord in the town, saw his long-dead neighbor walking up the steps of the Corn Exchange. His first wife parted the curtains of the psychiatric ward to watch the women coming out of the draper's shop in the street below. Even his Afghan hound loped around, loose downtown, though it had been mauled by junkyard dogs and put down eleven years earlier. It was not at all the vision he wanted, those he had cheated and harmed still alive, though not thriving. "Let's see something else," he said, and the magician tapped the glass again. His father threw dice, a woman leaning over him, her arms around his neck, while from the house next door could be heard the screams of the man's mother, giving birth to him. "Not that!" he said. The magician put the wand down and used his beautifully tapered index finger to set the clouds whirling within the glass. The man leaned in, everything obscure in the purple mist. He feared to see a tombstone with the date of his death, or thieves even now pulling all the cash and certificates out of his safe.

Dr. Montgomery showed Prenswick around his compound. Baboons dozed peacefully behind a bamboo fence. In another pen, a tiger lay by a boulder, taking in the evening breeze. Wide-eyed little lemurs climbed up and down dead trees hung with rope, inside a mesh enclosure. In the long wing of the L-shaped house, they knocked on a door. A young woman, her face calmly beautiful, looked up from her bed. Deep purple circles under her eyes troubled her smooth features, while her hair shone over her finely modeled shoulders. "How are you feeling, Gladys?" asked the doctor. She said no word, but smiled so beatifically Prenswick almost cried out, like a man climbing in the hills suddenly coming on some natural wonder, a rainbow, a white crag.

They left Gladys and met the few other patients, an older woman, a thin, pleasant man, both also speechless, features overflowing with an ancient peacefulness, like the very old, mellow in their chairs. "Nothing disturbs them," said Dr. Montgomery. "How they inspire me." But he coughed and turned his back when asked to explain what had been wrong with them, how they got to the island.

The doctor put Prenswick to work in the garden and doing some minor repairs around the estate. Gradually his strength increased. But at night, dreadful dreams washed over him. Always he was back in the boat, a huge wave about to crest, bringing with it the bloated faces of his two companions, the escapees from the disaster. Their dead hands, fingers puffed up like sausages, plucked at the knots tying him to the life boat. Though they were dead, they still spoke, "Prenswick, come with us." Every night Prenswick woke screaming, and though Dr. Montgomery injected him with a sedative, it only shoved the dream down for a while, where it paced uneasily below him, then surfaced as soon as the drug began to wear off.

"Can't you increase the dose?" he asked. The doctor obliged. During the day, he felt free of care, the sweat pouring down his back as he dug posts for a containment fence. The pleasant meals, the amusing animals, and the infrequent sight of Gladys walking in the distance with the doctor's assistant, corrected him, soothed him. They spoke only roughly of how he would continue his journey to Buenos Aires. The daylight hours melted around him, no clocks ticking, no deadlines, only a sense of physical accomplishment as he dug and carried, and the happiness of food and drink. Yet his nightmares increased in intensity, so that he became afraid to sleep, and lay with his eyes pasted open, sitting up against the wall, to fend it off.

The doctor celebrated his birthday with a fine bottle of champagne. His assistant, a dour, dark-faced hunchback who rarely spoke, acted as waiter at this meal, standing behind his master's chair with a white cloth draped over his arm. He poured the bubbly, and the doctor became unusually expansive. "What was the first domesticated animal?" he asked his captive guest. Prenswick had studied this at some point. "The bee," he said. "The Scots trained them to live in hives near our ancient dwellings. I attended a lecture on this last year."

"Interesting," said Montgomery. "But you are absolutely wrong. The first animal man domesticated was man himself." He talked about a philosopher Prenswick had never heard of, and explained how animals in the hunt are fully present to themselves and their environment. But man lives only for ideas, carrying out plans, moving forward in time in his ambitions, backward in his regrets. "We have made ourselves our own slaves," he said, musing over the rim of the champagne flute. "Always telling ourselves what to do. When are you ever free from the voices in your head, directing you, dear Prenswick?"

Prenswick didn't know how to answer. The drunken doctor leapt from his chair and lurched towards the hospital wing, ushering Prenswick with him. The assistant put out his arm and blocked Prenswick from following. Prenswick momentarily found himself inches from the face of the little servant, looking into the dog-like brown pools of his eyes. He saw something very cold there, and stepped back, stumbling to his room and blocking the door with the chair.

Yet later, he woke to a soft tapping. He opened, and a figure in white glided in, Gladys in a long nightgown. She put her arms around him, and in moments she was on top of him in the little plank bed. Her hair rained down around his face as her tongue opened his mouth. Like one long uninterrupted gesture his dick came erect and pushed its way inside her. She rode him in smooth ripples, her breasts brushing his chest. Her skin on his skin opened him up like questions answered one after another, ah, that's it, ah, that's right, ah, I understand, ah.

How did she know I loved her, he asked himself in the morning? She had left him sleeping, but the bed still smelled like her. He decided to leave the island, to go on to Buenos Aires when the supply steamer came by next, and to take Gladys with him. His mother and sisters would be overjoyed that not only was he alive and safe, but that he had married an adorable girl.

When he announced to Dr. Montgomery his intention to leave, his host became erratic. The assistant was always at his side now, pouring the wine, while also restraining the doctor, who began to ramble in his speech, and rant about the cruel, ignorant people who had run him out of London. He offered to cure Prenswick's nightmares permanently with a simple operation. "You need to wake up, you idiot!" he screamed. "I can wake you up!" He would not hear of Prenswick marrying Gladys. "You'll ruin her," he said. "She's perfect the way she is." He fumbled ruminatively with the pistol he now kept in his belt, while the assistant glared under his heavy brows.

Gladys came to him every night. They made love for hours,

never tiring, drinking each other in. He stretched out her palm and stroked her fingers when she lay nestled peacefully into his neck. During the day, just the sight of her heels in her slippers moved him. He longed for her mouth. While working in the garden he fell into reverie, reliving the way she had thrown her head and arms back when he pinched her nipple, arching against him. She had no reserve or resistance, but wanted him entirely.

The steamer arrived, put in the harbor for one day to unload. The captain dined with them. He slipped Prenswick a letter, from a family friend back home. "Your Dr. Montgomery," it read, "is a notorious murderer. He injected his patients with various animal hormones, which led to gruesome reactions. His botched surgeries, aiming to implant tiger and monkey glands, finally led to his arrest, but he escaped. Detectives hidden aboard the ship will capture him, once you and your fiancée are safe." Startled by the assistant coming up behind to take his plate, Prenswick let the letter fall to the floor. He picked it up, covering it with his napkin, but Montgomery and the servant had both noticed. "Let's see the menagerie!" said the captain, filling the awkward pause. Prenswick hurried to find Gladys, to urge her to pack her bag. They would board the ship as soon as it was dark. But her room was empty. He searched frantically, at last daring to burst open the locked door of Montgomery's laboratory. She lay strapped to a table, as white as if she'd been drained of all blood, a tube leading into her throat. On an adjoining table lay a white leopard, anaesthetized, fluids from its neck and groin running into beakers.

Back home in Scotland, the magician tapped the orb with his tapered finger. The man leaned in close to the whirling clouds beneath the glass. They covered everything, yet tiny flashes of light cut through, blips of fire signaling an elegant city, crystal palace, or a heap of diamonds, below the gloom. "I can't see," the man complained.

"You must focus," answered the fortuneteller. "Calm yourself and look."

The dark clouds dissolved, and he seemed to be looking down, from high above the earth. He barely made out the skyline of a city, bridges dotted with lights, candles gleaming on the packs of mules strung out on a mountain pass in twilight.

"Focus," said the magician. The man squinted down into the landscape, a sense of wonder pulsing up through him. This was his land, his future realm. If he worked very hard, was ruthless and untiring, in thirty years town, ocean, mountain, would be his. But with a blink the scene melted, as if the ring on binoculars had been turned, and only the lights were left, large and flowing into each other.

"What do you see?" asked the magician.

"Light," he said. "That's all. Please bring back the kingdom. I want to study it."

"What kingdom?"

"My kingdom, you showed me."

"This is all our kingdom," said the magician. "This is our future, every one of us."

The man bent himself closer, the moving lights pouring in through the shield of his lashes. The diamond brilliance of the orb concentrated into a white fire. Then it flashed a blinding, fatal brightness.

I wonder if Jonathan would forgive me for the wreck I've made of his lectures. "It's really a kind of thinking I want to get across," he explained to me many times. I was totally ignorant of his field, and tended to sink into my own concerns as soon as he delved into any kind of detail. "I want them to be able to consider the world around them," he said.

"Don't they do that already?" I answered, looking through the used car flyer that had come with the mail. Whatever he said next, I hummed over it, flicking through the coarse newsprint, my husband six inches from me only a sort of form, a conjunction of balding, kindly good intentions I neither looked at nor contemplated. He had already become a background, the two of us locked into our routines, careful that our interactions didn't cause too drastic a transformation. "What's that you said, sweetie?" I asked him a few minutes later. He was already on his way into the kitchen, where the cat complained about her empty bowl.

POLARITY

JONATHAN LUGGED HIS BRIEFCASE, bulging open, down the hall of the gray edifice where he'd worked for almost twenty years, and where I had gingerly accepted a temporary typing assignment from the employment agency I relied on. The first time he saw me, an unfamiliar face concentrating behind the department's monumental typewriter, he'd had a Styrofoam cup of coffee in one hand, the case of notes in the other. In order to free a hand to shake mine, a manly and businesslike formality that seemed to me totally unnecessary, he transferred the cup to the crook of his elbow. At last the free right hand shot out, while the burdened left side of his body tilted, and the cup dripped brown across his sleeve and into the mouth of the case. So he first appeared to me in the midst of an accident, and I sprang up to offer him the soiled brown paper towels I had earlier stowed on the window ledge to sop the drippings of the department's etiolated spider plant.

"Curses," he said, looking at the runnels of coffee disappearing into the papers. "But it doesn't matter." He told me his name, as if I should have recognized it, and I told him mine, with no expectation that he would ever remember the flimsy syllables that denoted my entity.

Amidst this next mess, some clear fragments: "The death of a baby, slave or stranger goes almost unnoticed. It arouses no emotion, occasions no ritual." The women of the tribe rubbed their hair on the coffins; these others cultivated yams whose vines had to be protected by sorcerers from incest and adultery; the members of this tribe dug up the corpses of their loved ones after three years of burial and whipped the decayed mess, lashed the remains with brutal leather thongs. "Only when we find the underlying oppositions can we make sense of this goulash of beliefs." The bones are masculine, the flesh is feminine, and so the corpse must be expurgated in this brutal fashion, before it can come to rest.

"Jenny," he said. "Of course," as if he already knew our story, had read it in a faulty translation years ago, had seen a bad movie adaptation of it in a hotel room in Tucson, so that it was somehow familiar, how he would meet his second wife, the good woman who would at last rescue him from the aimless disaster of his middle age.

Benjy, slide please. Caption, please. Focus. Can't read that one. You must have put your thumb right over it, Benjy, when you cleaned up last semester. All right, students, write down something with a J, pronounced "Y." It doesn't really matter what we call him. In any case, let's say Josefson traveled to Indonesia, to Tibet, through China and Russia, and found that all their so-called archaic peoples shared a story of a past state of continual communication between three worlds: the world above, the world below, and our mundane plane, hanging in between. Always these people proclaimed that in a prior age, their ancestors had easily passed up and down the axis of three worlds. In fact, the simple tent pole led up to the house of the gods. Little boys could climb it. And any wife loosening a few rocks or catching the tail of a duck could dive down into the world of the dead, a workaday world much like the world above, where smiths forged iron and women weeded the garden, a purple and gray garden under the earth, but a garden nevertheless.

Josefson was however deeply disappointed that the religions he investigated seemed in every case corrupted. Buddhist and Christian influences had seeped into them. The shamans looked blankly at him when he asked about the symbolism of the red threads they tied to birch trees, or why there were fifty-five good gods in the east and forty-four bad gods in the west. He already knew the answers to these questions, having been all over the planet and read, as well, every word published about primitive spirituality, even the naïve tales of female travelers. The struggle between the cultivated and the raw material, he wanted to say, the opposition of the known and the unknown, and always of course man against woman, gender being a container for all the other polarities, woman dark, man light, woman death, man life, woman sex, man procreation.

He fetched up in a far encampment somewhere between Russia and China, where in the right season the reindeer fed on red and white mushrooms and cavorted in ecstasy. The shaman, though, who was to cure a little girl, seemed dully ordinary. During the ceremony, he locked his face into a simulation of a trance, then simply fell asleep. "He's flying into the heavens to ask Aksa what's wrong with my girl," explained the child's mother. Josefson watched the man's throat pulse evenly, sure he was only napping. The hut was uncomfortably warm. He shifted his legs, but whichever way he sat, Josefson's knees ached. Hard traveling had done him in, and he hoped for a roomy office at the new technical college where he would be teaching come January. The shaman gave a little snort in his sleep, and set the cuff of his costume jingling. Josefson had asked him what the bells signified, and the man had only gaped at him. He had no idea that across much of the northern third of the globe, shamans wore bells to symbolize the voice of the unliving or mineral world.

The little girl, in a nest of furs, flushed with fever, also turned in her sleep, whining softly. Josefson watched her long lashes, partially gummed down with yellow encrustation. Sores dotted one side of her mouth. Abruptly the shaman sat up and looked around him fiercely. "Oh you demons," he said, "which one of you torments my little niece?"

Josefson wondered why he called out to the devils, when they lived under the ground. The sky, where the shaman had allegedly flown, was the home of either nine or seven divinities. The shaman stared at each corner of the tent, mumbling imprecations. "Oh, now I see," he said. "Yes, yes, it's very clear."

"The gods have given him an answer," said the mother. She had agreed to let the stranger watch the ceremony for a small sum. Her child didn't even seem particularly sick, or no sicker than many others Josefson had encountered. The day before, he'd seen a boy coming at him backwards, barefoot, dressed only in a little cape. Rickets had softened his bones so much that his legs had twisted in his hip sockets. His feet faced one way, his head another. His face, when Josefson spiraled around to catch a glimpse of it, was lit by a cheerful smile.

The shaman leaned over the sleeping girl and moved his hands in the air above her. He turned to his guest. "Give me your knife," he said.

Josefson fumbled in the cargo pocket of his coat and brought out his French clasp knife. He had shown it to the shaman earlier, its fine, simple design with the adjustable guard. The girl's mother began to whisper something quickly to the shaman. He was probably going to cut himself, to show that he was in a trance. Then he would draw out a bean or stick from the girl, and she would be well. One of Josefson's colleagues had published an account of a cure he had witnessed, where he had seen the shaman open the belly of the sick patient, all the guts momentarily exposed, and then close up the wound again so that there was no trace. Josefson became more hopeful. However the shaman, after opening and closing the knife once, noting its fine action, secreted it under a flap of his costume. After a few more minutes of gazing at the child, he sank back on his haunches, then returned to the floor and went back to sleep, assuring the mother first that the girl was recovered. The girl in fact began to stir and cry. The mother picked her up and sat her in her lap. Josefson was somewhat disgusted to see a child that size suck her mother's breast.

The whole stupid pantomime had been arranged to get the knife off him, he knew. He wouldn't be surprised if the shaman traded it to the Chinese for a bottle of their poisonous sap liquor. The flight to the heavens was a put-on just to secure the more usual trip to drunken numbness. He walked back alone towards the main part of the encampment. By the bend in the stream, he met a woman washing clothes. As she squatted on the bank, her long black hair covered her shoulders. The ends pooled on the ground and dripped into the water, some behind her, some in front of her. She wrung out a shirt and hung it over the branches of a low, spiny shrub. She must have heard his footsteps on the path, but she didn't turn towards him. Her hands glimmered palely beneath the broken surface as they scraped the cloth below the water. She wrung another out and turned again to hang it next to the others, this time drawing the whole curtain of hair up and over the opposite shoulder. Now he saw the baby resting in a sling on her back. Its little eyes bored into his curiously, judging him. Josefson shuddered and resumed walking.

"Sir," she called after him. "What did you see?"

"Very interesting," he said. "The girl is much better."

The woman laughed, and standing up, shed the baby sling. She lay the child on the ground near the drying clothes and gestured to him with one hand. She took his fingers and pulled him into the water. He followed her head first down a deep crevice, no light, the rock walls squeezing him, bursting his ribs, his heart pushing from the inside, the tunnel pulsing back, wailing and pressure in his ears. An immense heat scraped at him, as if trying to batter its way inside him, and only the ends of his fingers where she gripped him stayed cool. His desire to exhale met the heat, his breath battling to escape, the crushing force pushing to get in. What he was, Josefson, slimmed down to a tiny rind caught between the two. He would let his breath out and drown, or the cave walls would crush him, one or the other. And it didn't matter which. The little thing he was, was so insignificant. He sighed out his last earthly air, and found himself back on the bank, doubled over in the mud, vomiting.

She stood over him, still laughing. "Give me your knife," she said. He raised his chin, and a chain of vomit grew up from the ground, attached to the corner of his mouth. He felt it break and plop down, the stink of it emanating. "I already gave him my knife," he said.

"Don't you have another one?" Her face sharpened, the comely femininity angled now into intersecting planes, a holder for her scornful eyes.

Another one, he wondered? Where?

She leaned down to him, then wrenched at his pants. That one, there was the other one. But it wasn't at all sharp, until her hand throttled it. Then it was as if it jerked him into the air. She brought herself down on top of it, pushing his shoulders to lay him down, grinding his back into a rock beneath his spine. The rippling walls of her hair shut him into a dark tent. Her face looked down from the top of it, sky, as the earth pummeled him from below. In between, all that was left of his body squeezed into the sensations of his cock. Man action, woman reception, he thought. Man culture, woman wilderness. She leaned closer to him, her eyes half closed, exultant, absorbed. The flesh was feminine, the bones masculine. Like left and right, up and down, the schema of the human mind blossomed out of the directionality of the body, inescapable, unalterable. Yet was there perhaps a third thing, a mingling and sliding, an ungovernable something else? His whole precisely balanced edifice shredded and blew away as she brought her hands to his chest and pulled open the front of his shirt.

SNOWBALL EARTH

I'M GOING TO HAVE TO GO BACK and exclude the preceding lecture. His students wouldn't know what to make of it. Maybe it belongs to Man and Civilization, a course taught by another department altogether. Our concern here is with proto-humans, those shadowy beings who could only at most grunt and sigh. His students took his course, he told me, in order to earn their science credit, and considered him an entertainer, like a DJ at a graduation party, incidental to the real business of the night, which was the drinking and groping going on in the margins. Indeed, no one even listened to the guy their parents had hired, almost they felt sorry for him. Yet the DJ ended the evening with a check in his pocket, while the teenagers lay themselves down onto couches of doubt and insecurity.

After our dinner at Puff's, I thought Jonathan must have been disappointed in me, and I was relieved. I was fine the way I was. I didn't need him. He wasn't necessary to me. I didn't see him for two weeks. Late one afternoon he came in with two cups of coffee from the vending machine in the corner lounge. "Like some?" he asked. The cup he held out to me was ratty and dented, steaming feebly, the vaguely Greek-style insignia of the coffee company wallpapered all around its slick outer surface. He had come unaccompanied by his usual collection of papers, folders, library books. One cup he held back by his chin, and the other he centered between us, almost not close enough so I could take it. If I had shaken my head, he could have gone on, the second cup merely extra, to be chucked out, or given to someone else who would think nothing of it. He may even have drawn it back at the last moment if I didn't lunge for it eagerly enough. His eyes monitored my calculations, clicking through their own conclusions as I nodded, leaned forward, lifted my hand.

We each drank, him standing, me slouching behind my typewriter. I drained the brew, though he had put no cream or sugar in, it was not hot, and although a brown, bitter liquid, it didn't taste much like coffee. Its nastiness seemed directly proportionate to the humility of his gesture. I swallowed, each mouthful enchained to the next, an even, deliberate gulping. He finished his too, matching my pace, his pronounced Adam's apple bobbing up and towards me, then subsiding. I handed him the empty cup. As our eyes held over this transaction, everything was decided between us.

A travel writer received a post card from a friend from his childhood. The friend had gone to Peru to study the South American flamingo, and wrote of his stay in a highland village. He was startled to find ice islands in the Andean lake, as much as a mile long, and rising about 20 feet above the water's surface. "A good place for you to get an article out of," he wrote to his friend, while the geologists had already showed up to carbon date the icebergs, and found them the oldest in the world, outside of the polar regions. The writer's friend had previously urged him to do an Africa story that had won the writer a prize. They had sung in the choir together as boys, and now considered themselves nicely balanced collaborators, though they rarely saw each other. So the travel writer flew to Lima, then took a train and then a bus up into the mountains.

"Very nice," Professor Williams said, eying the stack of paper in my hand. "You've been working hard."

This of course was a compliment. They all worked hard and were proud of it, meetings scheduled back to back, always papers to grade, visitors to show around, galleys to proof, contracts with the teaching assistants and janitors to be gone over, little mock courts for students who had gotten sick but had not withdrawn and thus failed all their classes—these had to be presided over, and then letters written, stamps affixed, phone calls made to determine who was allowed to sign the document for the registrar, a fleet of young women with clipboards, of which I had been one, attending the gray but boyish clan of academic men.

I spoke to him on the porch, not wanting him to see the study. The shrubs out front bloomed in white and pink profusion, though the professor carried with him an indoor air of lamp-lit industry. I hoped I was not getting that way myself.

"Jonathan," he said. "I remember how surprised we were...." then he tutted, looking down, as if taking himself to task. "Well," he said.

"I know," I said.

He sighed, looking full in my face now. His feeling glance implied that Jonathan had been very happy with me, and perhaps that the reason was an enigma, or at least not obvious, because what could a man like Jonathan have seen in me besides my youth, which they were all sick of? They dealt in youth day in and day out, getting older while the new young ones replenished themselves in front of them, more like a natural resource than fellow humans. I could hardly have meant anything to Jonathan besides a sort of generic female complement, he seemed to say. Yet Jonathan had been transformed by my presence.

I sighed too, acknowledging the mystery of it all.

"The press has its own indexer," he said. "They send it out to her. You don't have to worry about that."

I remembered an afternoon when I had stopped by for Jonathan at the end of the day and we had met Professor Williams on the steps in front of the building. The two of them had talked on and on while I shifted my weight from foot to foot, invisible, mute. "You understood him so well," his department chair had said when he asked me to take on the editing of Jonathan's lectures. I had stood by as the two men discussed with gossipy intentness the wording or rewording of a letter or proclamation. Jonathan's hand on my arm lay leaden, while his face turned red and his voice rose. I had no idea what they were talking about, and it didn't occur to me to ask.

"Good," I said. "I wasn't sure."

"Just get the rest of it together. Mail it off. It will be fine."

"Thank you," I said. "You're such a help."

But he wasn't at all. Clearly I was misguided in what it meant to complete a set of lectures, and I wasn't going to get rid of it so easily. I wondered why I had called him, and why he had come, as overworked as he was, no free time at all. I was less and less willing to enter the study. Jonathan's tottering bookshelves, the floor mounded with envelopes, papers, and magazines, the desk weighed down with its scholarly cargo, seemed ever more capable of penning me in, the path to the door obscured behind me by a sudden fall of *Geophysical Annals*. I decided to bring Jonathan's typewriter out to the living room, but I couldn't lift the gigantic Selectric. I moved all the clutter off a tiny metal typewriter table, hoping to shift the behemoth from the desk onto this wheeled cart, and then tow it out to the other room, but thick rolls of dust and corrosion had gummed the wheels tight. They wouldn't revolve at all, the round rubber things more like strange paws than modern contrivances for mobility. The bearings within the wheels must have seized up, and I could see that if I continued to shove the little table, it would sooner fall over than roll.

I had to continue at his desk, with an ever more perilous stack of paper protruding from the black binder, including one heavily marked-over typescript. Entire lines had been blacked out, then "stet" written next to them, "stet" struck out and rescribbled atop it, "always," "even," "even though," and "still" alternating in heaps in one line that could not quite contain its conditional, "as if it would," "even though it still could," butting up against a black train wreck of inked-over clause. It seems fair, then, to make what I can out of this next section, the vacillations of optimism and dismay much more clear than the underlying signal: "that the Andean ice islands owe their survival to a covering layer of aragonite, an intensely white form of calcium carbonate that reflects most of the sunlight striking it."

At the last little town, where his friend had told him to hire a guide to take him up to the lake, the writer found a convulsion of carnival and market. Young men in black trousers etched with silver carried a feast on a plank through the streets, while boys sang and stamped. Women in gaudy costumes overran the town square, their overlapping blankets spread with trinkets. Confident, well-dressed tourists moved among them, stooping down to argue, holding pendants up to the light, dripping ice cream bought from the carts jostling the corners. The tourists were many of them as brown or only slightly less brown than the townsfolk. They had come from Lima and other cities, driven up for the week or unpacked from tour buses, which idled three deep in the street behind the hotel.

At the little coffee stand on the hotel porch, the waiter told him in clear textbook Spanish that the visitors had come for the tremendous bargains on silver jewelry. "You should get something nice to take back to your girlfriend," he said. "She'll be angry if you don't."

The writer smiled at the woman conjured up, pretty and petulant, putting her hands on his shoulders and shaking him. "You went all the way there and didn't get me a necklace?" He lived alone, and hadn't even had a dream about a woman in three years. Once recently he'd gone down to the laundry room in the basement of his apartment building and found the washer lined with a creamy white thing. He teased it out and stretched it between two hands to see what it was, a wet slip or nightie, sodden lace tilting over contoured cups that slackly indicated the breasts that had filled it. He clipped it to the clothesline between the dryer and some broken tables, feeling as if he had taken very good care. He could have wadded it up on the back of the washer. It hung in the dark basement for weeks. Then he went down one night and found it hanging by only one strap, shrugging asymmetrically. Someone had interfered with it, but not taken it away. It lay now in the back of his sock drawer, where its smooth silkiness sometimes startled his workaday groping hand.

The tourists, spending freely, saved tremendous amounts of money, as their every purchase was deeply discounted compared to what they would have spent at a jeweler's at home. Each trinket bought seemed to come packed up in a frothy layer cake of invisible money not given up, an etheric reckoning of money that might have been paid, as if large fortunes passed at the roulette table, the chips flashing by on the croupier's paddle, though the actual transactions involved handing over plain crinkled bills and receiving perhaps a little change. The indigenous women's little children toddled around with coins in their fists, then handed them to their brothers to buy sausages and roasted potatoes at the vendors' carts. The sound of haggling burbled underneath the distant treble of the boys singing in the churchyard. Girls in voluminous pink skirts came charging down the street, kicking and wailing, the fabric curling one way while their neat black boots flashed the other way. The travel writer felt nauseous and headachy from the thin air, but he refused to go back to the hotel and lie down. He had his own invisible currency, the money he would earn on his retailing of his adventure. He clicked his camera at the folk chorus.

The fate of the earth hung in the balance, Jonathan said. What is all this looking to the geological past, if not to fend off a horrifying end? Some of the geologists now claimed that the ice ages had been far fiercer than imagined, that at least once the planet had been thoroughly bundled in ice like a snowball, all its husk white and unfeeling. The glaciers were only toys, hardly aware of their power. When they at last dropped into the oceans, they had set off a terrifying chain reaction, cooling the sea water, bringing all to a standstill. When the sea itself froze, the abundance of minerals from sea creatures hung in tight lattices, bound to the water, and forming not the clear ice of freshwater lakes but the gleaming white calcinated ice. Its mother of pearl luster flung the sun's radiation right back in its face. It had taken only a few seasons to enter into it, but thousands to get out of. The sea ice refused to be warmed, and spread its coolness into the deep currents, like a virus in the blood. Seven thousand years later, the last remnant persisted in the Andes, so stubborn it couldn't be reasoned with.

"You didn't bring me anything?" the writer imagined his girlfriend saying. He told her about the llama, the mule, the bus, the lost bag, the bumpy air trip that filled the plane with the sound of retching and the aroma of vomit, how even he had felt like kissing the ground when they disembarked, as many of his fellow passengers did. "I missed you so much," he said, drawing her to him. Her head came right to his chin, so that what was most familiar to him was her scented hair tickling his lips. She sighed and held herself stiffly, as if enduring him. He had to put his hand on her chin to get her to tilt up to him so he could kiss her mouth.

"You didn't miss me?" he said.

"I only came over to say goodbye."

"But why? What's wrong? Is there somebody else?"

No, she said, no one, she was just sick of him, and sick of him being gone. He didn't care for her at all. He hadn't asked her to come along. When were they getting married? What use was it? The more she railed at him, the closer she came, until she was speaking into his chest, sobbing, telling him she couldn't stand him while her hands worked under his shirt. She pushed him onto the couch, where she pinned him under her, her wet face now pressed to his, hands in his hair. Then came a tremendous struggle to get out of their jeans, arms and legs arcing fruitlessly, fabric twisting and clinging, shoes tightly tied, feet wide and uncooperative, grunts of fury, until at last only one cuff clung to his ankle and he pulled her all the way onto him, a frantic sideways motion, fast anger, her groaning and digging her fingers into his arm, so tired, his body continuing its fight while his mind slid backwards to the marble humps thrusting out of the still water. It was only yesterday that he'd sat in the hut at the lake edge arguing in gestures with the fisher women, who insisted that they take a photo of him in their costume of wide hat and colorful vest.

"There is someone else," she said, once they were both quiet. An actor, a handsome man, though a little over the hill.

"You like him better than me?" he asked.

She didn't. He was so sweet at first, but he wasn't what he said he was. She'd gone out with him after a show, with all his friends. She thought she was going to drink with the leading players, but he took her to a table with the light crew and some other guy. He barely knew the cast. The other actors came by and slapped him on the back, but kept going, to the other end of the bar, while she and his gang occupied a table loaded down with expensive pitchers of English beer. She paid, because he didn't have any money on him, and neither did the others. He came home with her, leaning on her and crooning how beautiful she was. "Your skin is so creamy," he told her. "All the time in the bar I wanted to pull your shirt down and put my tongue right here." But he was the worst lover, so lazy, he'd hardly been paying attention, and then he passed out. In the morning, though, she said.

He didn't think he needed to hear it. "If that's the way you feel," he said, reaching for his shirt. But she clamped onto him, her legs over his legs.

"Don't leave me," she said. "You don't know." The actor had borrowed three hundred dollars from her. After that he wouldn't answer his phone. She went by the theater and they told her he wasn't there. She was sure he had told everyone at the door not to let her in. It was so humiliating. Even though it was no use, she'd gone by the theater every night for two weeks. Once she saw him in the distance, but he ducked down an alley to get away from her. Then he'd left a long message on her voice mail to tell her he loved her, that he couldn't stop thinking about her and he'd been waiting outside her building until she finally came home, but she hadn't showed up. "You're the one for me," he said. "You have to give me what I want."

He didn't remember her address, and had been staking out a similar apartment building a few streets over. She'd finally found him outside a little corner grocery, so drunk he could hardly stand. "And then," she said, but he really couldn't take any more.

"Why don't you know what you really want?" he said. "How can you tell me all this? How do you think I feel?"

"How do you think I feel?" she said, and it hung between them as they looked into each other's faces, all that they didn't know and couldn't figure out compressed into the few inches that separated them.

MAN AND DESTINY

THE LECTURE STARTED a few minutes late that morning. Perhaps he'd lingered in bed with his new wife. No, the students say. He had an argument with her. Look how red his eyes are. But no, I can't imagine the students knew or cared anything about his personal life. Please settle down, he told them. Publishing back and forth in their journals, he said, harruming behind the lectern, the scholars wondered endlessly how man managed, after standing up and walking about, to develop such a magnificent brain case. Slide please. Even from these hundreds of scattered chips and bone shards, they've resurrected something resembling a skull, and from its inside made castings of the traces left of the interior arteries, calculating from one minuscule stretch of it this being's blood pressure, blood volume, brain volume, and its capacity for thought. Why think at all, he said, looking into the crowd of youths, all their heads tipped down towards their notebooks, twirling their rings, chewing their pencils, drawing zombies and masked men, whispering to their fellows, "Did you see Sarah yesterday?" and "What happened to Nick last night?" Suppose, he said, as most of them do these days, that man's hunting ability drove the increase in his brain's size and capacity. Hunting entailed his need to communicate by yodeling articulately across the savannah, his need to predict future movements of the herds of prey, and indeed one particular prey's future motion over the next few seconds as he plots the trajectory of his wooden spear. You can't imagine, Jonathan intoned, the chapters and chapters dedicated to this hypothesis, the mathematical complications enacted by hunting activity, the social cues required, the increase in cubic centimeter of brain mass our ancestors needed in order to kill and butcher. Slide please. This chart, he said, is a good example.

The students stared stupefied at the ghastly ranks of numbers. Each set of digits hung transfixed by a decimal point like a dagger piercing a dead man's neck, pinning him to the stockade wall. Though thought, consciousness, language, are the most ephemeral of phenomena, we can get closer to them through applied mathematics, he said. We do not postulate without evidence. It's really a kind of thinking I'd like them to take away, Jonathan said to me more than once, while I picked at my cuticles or wondered how the orange juice pitcher could be so well hidden in the back of the fridge. Thinking? I said cheerily.

His gruesome chart was probably meant for the advanced seminar. It slipped into the undergraduate lecture series by mistake. He would have taken Benjy to task, though it must have been his own error, and continued on with his explanation of primal aggression, or skipped to some other topic, pottery, shamanism, how the vegetal has disappeared from the fossil record except in the case of abrasion marks and what can be deduced from petrified turds.

Of course I have my own idea about what fits here. I don't see why *Geophysical Annals* couldn't make room for some of the lighter reading I whiled away the hours with as I ventured to keep Jonathan company in the early days of our marriage. One evening, Jonathan could easily have said to the fidgety students, the noted physician Dr. Jackson swept past his butler and locked himself into his laboratory. "I am not to be disturbed," he called over his shoulder. Even if he did not come out for days, no one was to look for him. Do not break down the door, the doctor said. If you hear anything strange, please pay no mind. All this the butler told to Dr. Jackson's lawyer, a few weeks after Dr. Jackson's disappearance. The doctor went out on foot in the most frigid weather, wouldn't take his carriage, and came back with many parcels and boxes packed with straw, the name of a chemical supplier stamped across them. The smells that came out of the laboratory sometimes sent the whole staff behind their handkerchiefs, corpses and flowers, sulfur, and a scent the maid described as intensely blue, though who knows what she meant by that. Then one evening the smell changed absolutely. The rotting note shifted to something slinky and animal, while the overriding odor resembled a May evening, all the apples and lilacs in bloom up and down the avenue. The butler heard the door slam, and he presumed the doctor had gone out the back way, where the laboratory exited into the alley. He had all the keys to Dr. Jackson's house except that one.

Man the hunter, Jonathan said, and none of you have even squawked. I'm ashamed of you. It's as if while the men were out stalking, the women sat on the ground immobile, as if they were formless blobs. All this brain activity, language, trajectories, has been posited over and over to men, as if man evolved, and then every now and then reached into some kind of closet, cabinet, and took out a woman, the dusty old thing, primitive, out of style, and did what with her? Time after time they glue one of these brain cases together, foist their formulations on it, and pronounce, voila, a man, ancient man, surrounded by his weapons. When will we see a woman, surrounded by her tools? Slide please. Never. Believe me, I've searched for a single such illustration.

Here he showed a nursemaid pushing a pram, a high, Victorian baby carriage, the child obscured by a funereal black hood. I'm ashamed of you, he said. You should know better.

The girl in the central row looked down, not sure what he was saying but made uncomfortable by it. Her companions whispered and blew their noses. No matter. The newspapers filled with stories of a remarkable chanteuse, classy Miss Jay, who had come out of nowhere to warble down at the Emerald Club. The newspaper illustrator's inky caricatures hardly did her justice, all who had seen her in the flesh said. She's enchanting. Bewitching. Dr. Jackson's friend De Martin settled into an armchair in the late afternoon to list off her charms, her neck stretched up just before she sang, the pang of her first note, the sulky way she cast her eyes down at the end of the song. She had come and sat at his table for a little while, DeMartin said, and he had taken her hand.

The doctor sat up, smoking agitatedly. De Martin hardly noticed. He had run his fingers up the inside of her arm, he said, and had the feeling that never had a woman been so alive. "You've got to see her," he said. "Come with me tonight. I've persuaded her to come out with me afterwards, for a bite at Donovan's."

"Tell me about her arm again," the doctor said. "What was it about it, exactly?"

"You know how women are, old boy," he said. "So coy. Always withdrawing. As soon as you approach, they draw back. You draw back, they get up their nerve and shrink forward, you know, so trussed up in their reactions. Miss Jay, though. When my fingers were on her arm, it's as if nothing else on earth existed for both of us. And her skin was so warm."

He sank back in the chair, remembering.

"Her scent, too," he added. "Nothing like it in the world."

"Yes, yes," Jackson said, standing and shooing his friend out the door. He rushed into the lab, where the staff heard again the shufflings of glassware and smelled the tannery odors. The butler knocked at dinnertime, but got no answer. He heard a

94   Angela Woodward

cry, as if in surprise, or of passion, but only a single note. Then the scent curled through the keyhole, tuberoses and lilacs, underpinned with panther and amber. The back door thudded, the one in the alley, and the house exhaled, now empty of its master.

We find these skeletons, Jonathan said, slide, please, and assume from the amount of ornamentation left circling their bones, that these are the remains of men of authority. This gigantic golden penis, he said, was found, he said, while the crowd of students rippled in anxiety. Did he say penis? They peered at the screen, but couldn't make out from the gray, thickly lined illustration any hint of sensuality in the artifact depicted. Abbe Breuil, who had carefully cataloged thousands of cave paintings, was horrified to see the way his fellow Frenchmen explained them, every ox a man intent on trampling and goring the horse-woman. He, pain inflicted, she, pain enduring, depicted in the depths of the caves for 40,000 years, our most long-lived human culture, according to the French academy, based on a fundamental pivot of man the sadist and woman the masochist. Every pointed thing became a penis-spear, while the idea that they could have been branches, twigs, beautifully observed parts of plants, was poo-pooed.

"Why didn't you come by and see Miss Jay with me last night?" Dr. Jackson's friend asked. DeMartin noted the deep circles under his friend's eyes, the dissolute stubble on his neck. Dr. Jackson looked like he had been burning the candle at both ends, but DeMartin knew he was too sensitive to abide that being mentioned. He told the rapt doctor again about Miss Jay's warmth. "One touch," he said. "And I've never been so excited. She hardly spoke to me, but I felt completely in tune with her, as if she could read my thoughts."

"And then what?" asked the doctor, as DeMartin lapsed into reverie.

"Her scent," DeMartin said. "It's as if it exudes from the core of her body. It's not on her skin, it's her essence, the most purely feminine ... she pulled me down on the bed ... her mouth ... she... ." Flustered, DeMartin got up and looked for his hat.

"You made love to her," the doctor said, also rising. He stood over DeMartin, his reddened eyes squinted down to an uncomfortable small bore. "Or she made love to you? It was mutual. Like you never dreamed was possible, her bucking under you, sucking you in, climbing on top of you, pushing you down, pulling you to her, right? Wasn't it like that?"

DeMartin, ashen, couldn't answer. The doctor's feverish, unpleasant intensity repelled him. He left, and Dr. Jackson returned to his lab. He mixed his chemicals, set them boiling, siphoned off the foam, watched the colors change, and at last, the precise moment, the hinge point, he drank it down. He staggered to the mirror, where the clear brown eyes of Miss Jay looked out at him, man's coat and collar incongruous. She tore off the doctor's clothes and poured the black cocktail dress over her head. Transformation complete, she slammed out the back door and made for the café where she had agreed to meet her new lover.

Even the tattle pages were afraid to more than hint, until it struck the inside metro news: the singer had arranged an orgy at an exclusive hotel, and escaping, had been seen in the most lurid brothel districts. One columnist speculated that the young woman had a fatal disease, and was experiencing men before she died. She'd been spotted down by the docks, hair alive in a froth around her head, black skirt slapping her ankles, pulling behind her a lusty sailor. A medical man weighed in about the romantic frenzy that sadly afflicted females who were not strapped down into marriage early enough, a well-known medical fact, but one that bore repeating. DeMartin came to Dr. Jackson completely downcast. "She was so pure in her touch," he said. "I can't describe it. I thought it was only me she wanted. In fact I still believe it. I know what passed between us."

Now she was a hunted woman, accused of debauchery and corruption. Worse, an old man had died in her embrace. It's possible she would be hanged. If he only knew where she was hiding, the doctor's friend said, he would help her. He didn't care what they said she'd done. "When I'm in your house," he said, gazing at Dr. Jackson's shoes, "I can somehow think about her peacefully. When I'm home, I'm like an animal."

The doctor shivered. The butler came into the room with more whiskey. As the servant disturbed the air currents in setting down his tray, a fine floral essence circulated, then disappeared. "What's that smell?" DeMartin asked. Dr. Jackson sprang up and made sure the laboratory was locked. Pushing his friend out the door, he curled onto the leather daybed in the lab, pressing his hands to his temples. "How can I do it?" he said. His dearest wish was to make love to Miss Jay, as Dr. Jackson, but he could not do it, as he was both. He wanted to thrust himself into her, and simultaneously feel what she felt, which was ten, a hundred times what he had ever felt himself. He wanted to press down on her chest, feel her breasts sliding against him, while also feeling his own hairy weight locking onto her as she pushed up and in. He had never had such joy as that encounter down at the docks, when the man had simply bent her over a chair. So now he could do the same, to some woman who would hold still for it, but how could he enter Miss Jay, alive and vivid to her core? He wanted to feel what she felt, while feeling what he felt. "Such unity is impossible," he said to himself. And what a tragedy, he thought. Before, he'd never noticed that women had any passion at all.

"Really, you won't protest?" Jonathan said. "We are after all constructing a whole world from such partial evidence as this." The ornamented skeleton stared down at them from the screen. The caption now contained the word "so-called" before "man of authority," as further molecular analysis had suggested the bones were female. The students burrowed into their seats. Only a few years earlier, the campus women's caucus had sent a delegation to the provost's office, demanding the change of all the courses with "Man" in the title: Man and Destiny, Prehistoric Man, Man and Civilization. The provost had patiently explained that it was only a matter of grammar, irrefutable and completely neutral, that woman was subsumed inside Man and Destiny, that in fact she was right there, fully a subject of inquiry, couldn't they see that? "Actually it's 'man' that's inside 'woman' if you look at the spelling," one of the students said. The provost scoffed. That wasn't it at all. Man was the universal, woman only a particular. At last he had brought the registrar out to explain that course name changes couldn't be processed without protracted negotiation and significant cost. They must take into account all the index cards that would have to be typed over again, this work carried out by a bevy of silent secretaries, unseen in basements and dim hallways from one end of the college to the other. So impractical, these students, the provost mused. They had no consideration for others at all.

SILENCE

THE EXISTENCE OF THIS FEATURE indicated by a one, the non-existence of this feature indicated by a zero, on and on down the center of the page. The gray inset box holding Figure 1 thrust behind it the pale, orderly black and white of the rest of the page. The lines of text, obediently stretching from one margin to the next, seemed cowed by the solid box, so dense in its tiny type. Asterisks ornamented it, as well as tiny, down-held swords, like the paraphernalia of an infant prince. Jonathan's study contained multiple copies of this, his opus on jaw measurement. The black binder gaped open around three issues, one pristine, one dog-eared, the other folded back on itself so that the staples bowed out and snagged my hand. They shoved themselves out from the book shelf, too, and slumped across a leather in-tray. The press must have sent him reprints to give to his friends and family, or to hand out to his colleagues and students. Jonathan knew the name of every socket that held a tooth or proto-tooth. The stretches of jaw near the chin, near the ear, and all in between, were also not anonymous segments of bone but officially recorded pieces of anatomy, their starting and stopping points agreed upon. But few people were able to hold to these agreements. His jaw research was so specialized that only a handful of people on earth could apprehend and comment on his work.

We proceed only when the evidence tells us to, he said, and based on the evidence of your last exam, we should stop now. I don't believe you're even listening.

Maybe if we had a textbook, the students grumble, instead of these dingy xeroxes. One of my predecessors had typed the class notes years ago, then run them through an ancient, hand-cranked mimeograph machine. At some point, the faded mimeo sheets had been pressed onto the glass of a photocopier. The many iterations blurred the type, filled in the dots of the e's, chopped the ends of words off at the margins where the secretary's hand slipped on the copier. But the notes are only an organizational aid, he tells them. Students are to rely on what they themselves write down during the lecture, because here he'll cover everything they need to know. Pay attention and you'll do well, he said.

He had promised them at some point an explanation of the decline of the megafauna. The animals we know today are only dwarves compared to the mammoth, the mastodon, the dire wolf, the glyptodont and Irish elk. These massive creatures all died off as the last of the ice retreated. That is, when conditions warmed, became more pleasurable, they suffered. The earth of today is *unimaginably different* from that of our recent past, he said, a note the students had made dozens of times already, that they had underlined and scribbled rings around. Benjy put up slide after slide, museum paintings, in almost all cases showing the animals in their death throes. An archaic camel raised its neck from a tar pit that swallowed its body. A saber-toothed cat slashed at an attacking eagle. Woolly mammoths marched in a line into deep snow from which it was unlikely they would ever emerge. Jonathan looked down at his notes while Benjy flipped through more paintings of an assortment of flightless birds.

One student came in late, tucking her coat around her as she squeezed past her mates for an empty seat in the middle. All the heads swiveled back to take her in. The auditorium door swung shut behind her with a dry clang. The breeze from the closing door brushed their cheeks. When they looked back to their notebooks, they read again that the earth of today is unimaginably different from *indecipherable*. A sort of spirit flew around the room as the latecomer unwrapped her scarf from her neck and dug through her bag for a pen.

The existence of this feature marked by a one, the non-existence of this feature marked by a zero, through the whole catalog of features, many more than you would think for six inches of bone. The point was to establish ratios, so that other ratios could then be hypothesized, whether this creature or that creature had the proper physiology to produce language or only grunts and sighs. My now late mentor Wilson, he said, developed this approach, which I have further refined. Let me give you an example, he said.

On the screen, a cave bear stood upright, shaking its scimitars at what might be primitive jackals.

What if, he said, language had only two words, "ah" and "oh"? The existence of this thing confirmed by "ah," the non-existence of any other thing signified by "oh." When a bird rose in the forest with a sudden loud beating of wings, its observer said "ah." The baby crawled too close to the fire, and the mother scolded, "ah." Each utterance referred back to myriad others, the fire, the bird, the left, the north. Then everything that wasn't— longing, solitude, silence—could be summed up by "oh." When we expect to see her face, but it turns out she hasn't come to the party at all, "oh." At this point we have only to measure which is greater, the existence of things, or the non-existence of things.

The woman scuffled in her bag, bringing out another notebook. Apparently the first one had been for another class. She opened it on her knees and flipped through the pages for her stopping place. The tiny fluffing sound of the paper accompanied the dust motes hanging in the beam of the projector in the black interval between slides. She pulled the flat desk surface, tucked away in the side of every auditorium seat, up and open. The hinges protested weakly. The sound of their muffled screech commanded more attention than the man behind the lectern. The people to her left and right all turned their heads to her, though she in the center seemed completely unaware. Jonathan ceased to speak, but her pen moved, this too sending out its little note, scritch scritch, a tune completely unrelated to the words and phrases it drew the symbols for.

Here, he said, we have, he said. On the screen, a mound of carcasses steamed in a lurid dawn. The hunters had driven the whole herd of bison off a cliff, and butchered only the top two or three out of the thousands killed. We have only to weigh, he said, the nonexistent things against the existent things, whether the imponderables outnumber the graspable, enumerated objects and actions. Why don't we think about this awhile, he suggests? The students fidgeted, checked their watches, whispered to each other. Only the woman who came in late still wrote, her hand moving methodically left to right, then returning. She must have filled several pages already, the pen's dry tune steady and vigorous. All the heads on the left side of the auditorium swiveled to the right, while all those on the left turned the other way. Those in front swung around behind, and those in the back rows peered down. The boy in the projection room stayed his hand. Jonathan leaned on his arms on the lectern, his glasses down his nose. A current billowed under the rafters. It may have been the absent, the uncreated, the dead, but there was no way to know. Maybe it was only unease. The students tapped their erasers on their desktops, yawned, and scrabbled in their backpacks for gum. Only the one continued writing, oblivious, filling the silent hall with the intensity of her concentration.

LISETTE

TODAY WE WILL INVESTIGATE BOGS, he said. Of course the students will have to remain in their seats, but I'll have him take them on an imaginative journey to the fringes of France. Despite the bickering that went on all around it, one brown-green corner of Alsace had slept unplumbed for 140,000 years, Jonathan said. A botanist laid some slices of it under her microscope to observe the fossil pollen trapped in the peat. At the bottom, in the earliest layers, she found hornbeam and alder, mild, pleasant trees of a temperate climate. On top of this, she found spruce, more and more over what looked to be a span of about a century. The bog must have cooled, so that as many years passed, this cold-loving species eventually predominated. Then over what seemed a stretch of only twenty years laid out in the annual layers she had been counting, the type of vegetation shifted sharply. Over these two decades, the bog had become only sparsely populated, and this entirely with tundra species found some thousand miles to the north.

She returned home, where her husband had made dinner. "How's little Madeline?" she said. "I'm sorry she's already asleep," he told her. "She has something to show you tomorrow." She forgot to ask him what it was. And the next day, she set off for Paris early to confer with her old professor. A sudden tumble into an unsurvivable winter, she said she'd found. They had supposed that climate change had been and would be gradual, but this was a disaster. The speed of the conversion was here accurately recorded in her data. Only twenty years, as if from childhood to adulthood, and the earth could go from chilly to barren. We ought to warn people, she said. We can't depend on anything.

The professor told her that her results were mistaken, though he knew her to be exceedingly punctilious. He asked her to confer with his colleague Bernard. He wrote a letter to Dr. Bernard on her behalf, and then they went out for coffee. They spoke about his daughters, and her little one, and his garden, and the properties of lichen. It was not one plant, but two combined, a symbiosis of an algae and a fungus. They grew together, extremely slowly, enduring the most inhospitable conditions. Is that so, she said?

Bernard failed to send a reply. She spent the night in her professor's house, then went the next afternoon to visit the great man in his laboratory. On the way, she walked through the neighborhood on the fringes of the hospital, where all the medical students lived. Horrendous groans and cries seeped out of basements and garrets. The students practiced their technique on dogs, binding them and slicing them up, laying bare their nerves. Some of these flayed beasts had been casually strewn in the alley. Their bodies, stiff, pale, often with missing limbs, jaws, ears, would have demonstrated the arrangement of their muscles if they had not been completely obscured by flies. The dead dogs had ceased suffering, though the students would have maintained that the live ones too did not suffer, only reacted. Their unearthly cries were only a kind of symptom, like the sound of glass breaking.

It's all a question of balance, Jonathan said. It's true, according to our best calculations, that we are headed towards another glacial era. Changes in the earth's orbit since 5,000 years ago, when the temperatures of the interglacial peaked, have been in a direction that favors the growth of ice sheets. Even within our lifetimes, it may be that we wake up in a freezing bed, our toes so cold we can hardly walk across the room to turn on the little space heater, and yet it's July. As we cut forests in the northern hemisphere, we create flat fields where winter snow lies naked under the sun, blandly reflecting away all the heat rained down on it. Thus human activities demonstrably foster conditions for increasing cold. But at the same time, other human acts release gases into the atmosphere. These may help us retain some heat, and so counterbalance or delay our inevitable slide towards glaciation. We are building even now complex models of the earth and all its elements, past and present, in order to predict our future outcome. We must think always what our own actions can achieve, what our efforts can produce, he said.

The botanist hurried through the narrow streets bordering the hospital, her head down. Even though her eyes focused only on her shoes, jumbles of removed veins, turd-like organs, eyeballs, testicles affronted her from the pavement. Brown blood crusted the cracks between the cobblestones, and from left and right, above and below, came the keening and whimpering of the vivisected victims. In her fluster, she missed her turning. She stopped, knowing she had gone too far, and looked around her. A young man came towards her, smiling. "Can I help you?" he asked.

"No, I'm fine. I've missed my street, but I'll find it. Thank you."

He tucked his hand around her elbow. "I know you," he said. "We met last week, at Barzac's party."

She had taken a step with him, while shrugging her arm away. But he kept his grip. "You're mistaken," she said. "I see my street. I'll be going. Thank you."

"I know who you are," he said. "I recognized you straight away. I'm David. You remember? We talked. But only for a little. Maybe I didn't make much of an impression."

She turned her head to look at his face, and found his forehead wrinkled, a sad, innocent perplexity. She felt sorry for him, and spoke more kindly, telling him again he was mistaken. She told him the name of the street she was looking for. It was right back there, he said. He would take her to the corner. She didn't want his company, but she relented, since she'd already offended him, and he seemed sensitive. "You're a student?" she said. He was pursuing his medical degree, but human nature was his real interest. It didn't do much good to know how pumps and mechanisms worked in the particular, if you didn't understand the place of human beings in the grand scheme of things, their behavior and dreams, their inner motivations. "There's your street," he said. "You went quite a ways past it. You must have been lost in thought."

She thanked him and went on, but he called her back. He wanted to show her something. "Look," he said, pointing through a basement window.

In those same bogs, Jonathan continued, which have been such a rich source of data about past vegetation, whole Viking ships have been found, perfectly preserved. Bodies, too, have come to light, tanned by the acidity of the peat, but in every other respect life-like. Thousands of years old, they look like they died yesterday, as if no time at all had passed. Benjy, slide please. The bog man looks like the finest statue, carved in pewter. Even the stubble of his beard is just as it was in life, and the wrinkles on his cheeks. His expression of extreme serenity is at odds with the noose around his neck. The rope, too, has retained all its detail, every fiber natural and complete, the peculiar bog environment having kept all of him exact, just as he was when thrown into it.

The botanist stood next to the medical student, peering down where he pointed. She would indulge him for a minute, since he seemed to need her kindness. In the dim, narrow street, it took a while for her eyes to focus to see through the dirty glass. "Ah Lisette," he said. "I remember you just like that, last week." A dog hung upside down from a winch, head down over a table. Leather straps held its back legs to a hook. Its whole front hung exposed, open and undefended, ready to be touched, tickled, shaved, or sliced into. A black mask covered its snout, holding its mouth shut. The eyes looked into hers, mutely appealing.

"I'm not Lisette," she snapped, whirling on the young man, flinging his arm off. He snatched at her wrist and kissed it. He laughed into her furious face, and she saw herself as he saw her, naked and helpless, a confection for his use. Here was someone who could bind a woman, gag her, and set the chain that hoisted her slightly swinging as he and another one sucked her nipples. Even slapping him wouldn't change his perspective, but she did it anyway. Her face was still marred with tears when she knocked on Professor Bernard's door.

He refused to see her. He had indeed received her mentor's note, but he had no use for female scientists. Her data was surely wrong; it wasn't even worth a consultation. She didn't have the strength and intellect to look through a microscope. Moreover, he considered her neither man nor woman, he had the maid say to her. She was an aberration. Such an unnatural creature he could not address himself. Her calculations were surely rot, and she should go back to her baby.

GAIA

THIS LAST WAS A LITTLE TOO HARSH for the students. After all, they've only signed up to earn their science credit. A plain depiction of the three types of rocks, a little note on geologic time, and a few slides of mastodons would do them nicely. They have no need to consider the complications of human beings, and should only mark on their quizzes whether this or that species of hominid left chemical traces of phosphorus or manganese. Jonathan's more astute students have managed to sketch out a few conflicting theories about the earth's climatic shiftiness. The bulk of them have gathered a few ringing phrases, such as that the earth of today is *unimaginably different* from the world of the past, though this seems to them both self-evident and unimportant, hardly worthy of this protracted weekly lecture. For all I know, they're doing their Spanish homework when they appear to be most diligently taking notes on Jonathan's material.

Let us consider the earth and all her inhabitants as one entire living organism, Jonathan said. It's an unconventional way of thinking about it, he said, the Gaia hypothesis. Everything belongs. The earth's animals inhale what her plants exhale. The wind shimmers the leaves of the birches, the frogs speak to the darkness. The vole belongs to the tunnel, the tunnel to the vole. Sand and snow, potassium, juniper, ocelots, reptiles, by maintaining their differences, fulfill their various roles. Just as you students have toenails and aortas, distinct in their form, texture, and function, so the earth has volcanoes, shrews, sinkholes, and forests, all acting in concert. They influence the atmosphere and the ocean currents in various ways, maintaining the entire earth system, climate included. We don't posit a directing force, but hold that the biota act unconsciously to shape the earth for *optimal life conditions*. Of course it's only a theory, Jonathan said. I'm not sure what kind of experiment would prove it. Or what the point would be. Benjy, he said, move on, please.

Benjy coughed in the projection booth.

Benjy, keep awake up there.

The slides haven't been put in order this morning. He should have numbered them and stacked them, for the boy to insert into the carousel ten minutes before class. Notations on his outline should have indicated where the next slide went, so that voice and image coincided, reinforced each other. But the system has broken down a bit. The problem is that Jonathan has died, and left me here to make sense of all this. I was struck by the lichen in the previous lecture, its partnership of unlike creatures. I wished that he had pointed that out to me, taken my hand and shown me the gray and yellow scales covering an old wall at the end of the garden. In fact the garden has no wall but is backed by the neighbor's garage, a bright red faux barn housing lawn tools and a second fridge of cool pop. Jonathan didn't even know their names, the family living behind him, and I've continued his tradition of saying hello to them and nothing more, whenever they cross my path.

I took some pages from the black binder out into the garden. Though Jonathan isn't here to look after them, the plants seem to have done well for themselves anyway. I can't name any of them except the dandelions, but swords and flags sun themselves, topped with white and purple spreading faces. He would have put in a long line of those glossy pink ones, low along the bottom, maintaining order. Now there's no sort of break at all between the garden and the lawn. Jonathan might have been irked with me, but I prefer it this way.

Benjy, he said, let's get on with it.

A formation of Roman soldiers bristles across the screen. No, no. That's from next semester, what used to be called Man and Civilization, taught by another department entirely. This is Earth and Prehistory, where we have no civilization, just tiny foraging bands of proto-humans. Did they speak, he asks his assembled students? Or only grunt and sigh? The students grunt and sigh in reply, looking down into their notebooks, or simply at their hands.

A man lost his wife to a fever, and lived on alone in their house, as they had no children, he said. His neighbors dropped in on him with their female cousins, the daughters of distant friends. His sister trawled through her acquaintances, even stopping women she saw in the market, thinking their faces might be the kind the bereaved man would respond to. But he turned down all these suggestions without considering them seriously. He was still in love with the deceased, they all concluded. Once he finally got over her, he would come around. He needed someone to help out with the vineyard, and it was important to have an heir.

The man had a new love, hidden from them all. Even while his wife was still alive, he'd seen her sometimes, and mused on her. She was a wasp who flew in his kitchen window and buzzed against the pane. She rarely looked around, and he couldn't think that she'd ever noticed him. But she must have felt his stare. She was so neat in her habits, so self-contained, and her narrow waist and long legs trailing behind her seemed to him the utmost of feminine charm. Her elegant proportions, her smart wardrobe, and her air of detachment made her linger in his thoughts. When his sister displayed for him some new friend, thick in the ankles, shy under her bonnet, he could only think of the delicate wasp. She was far lovelier than his sister's acquaintance, or any human woman. He laid a bowl of water in the yard for her. She balanced on the edge, then dipped down over the water. She flew away without thanking him, but he thought she might have given him a look of acknowledgement, a tiny glint from her hard eye.

This is hardly science, but only a fairy tale, a critic wrote, shortly after the book on the earth's systemic interconnectedness, the Gaia hypothesis, came out. We'll operate as if it's the book, said Jonathan, and not its author, that caused the furor. The biota produce the books, but the books have a way of making themselves felt through their own manipulations, words spawning more words, a life system of their own. Immediately, religious figures claimed the book. This is our new cosmogony, wrote one of Abbe Breuil's followers. It makes plain that the earth is evolving through stages of *cosmogenesis*. That word preened itself, a particularly powerful specimen, or maybe only a vain one. Because the book named its theory for a Greek goddess, Gaia, other books impugned it, saying it had meant all along to put a spiritual spin on its thin masquerade of earth science. The land and the oceans, whispering to each other "warmer, colder, warmer, colder," in a continuous feedback loop between ecosystem and climate, they found distastefully romantic. Yet they had known for forty years already that the oxygen, nitrogen and carbon dioxide in the atmosphere had been put there by living creatures. As usual, signees at conferences found for or against. A thousand assembled in London to issue support to Gaia, while ten thousand more, at scattered meetings, either denounced vociferously or dismissed the topic without debate. It had a kind of stain to it, a perfume of femininity and the occult.

The widower at last prayed to Venus to bring him closer to the wasp woman. "I don't ask for marriage, just to have her listen to me. Let me tell her what's in my heart. Only this much, I beg you!" Venus had rarely had such an unusual request. Once a man had asked that his pretty white cat be turned into a woman. Venus bestowed this wish, but the recipient was horrified when his cat-wife leapt out of bed in the middle of the night and caught a mouse. If he had truly loved her, he would have left her how she was. The goddess considered what to do in the widower's case. One problem was that her little son Cupid hated wasps. One had stung him once, and he had run to her howling. "How much more do your arrows hurt those mortals you prick!" she told him. This didn't console the child. So though the goddess heard the man's prayer, she ignored it. It was safer. There wasn't much she could do, and she didn't have to do anything.

Having prayed, however, the man trusted that Venus had worked some transformation for him. He sat by the water bowl and waited for the wasp to return. Eventually she lit on the edge. The water sparkled, cool under the hot sun. The wasp rubbed her hands and looked down into it. "Pretty lady," the man said, "I know you can hear me. I want you to know how much I admire you." The wasp skimmed over the water two or three times. He watched her, but wasn't sure how she drank. She may have gathered the water up beneath her, or she dipped her mouth into it so discreetly he couldn't see it. The air hummed with the beat of her wings. The widower listened to this noise, with all the bird song, warble and chatter set in the background. The summer day could not have been more beautiful. He imagined the wasp accompanying him on a circuit of his fields, sometimes nodding to comments he made. The peace of her companionship, just to turn his head and see her near him, soothed him. The wasp circled the water bowl once more and flew off, coming close to his face as she left, and giving him, so he thought, another hard little glance, as if measuring him. "Ah!" he said. He was sure already that he loved her. Maybe one day, she would love him too.

The book of Gaia continued its dialog with other books, reviews, journal articles, forewords and citations. If the biota have evolved in response to the environment, then the environment too has evolved with the biota, it said. Thereby it linked its hypothesis with a grand theory, and claimed kinship with that earlier work of another biota, Charles Darwin. It posited a transcendent circularity, the actions, gases and excretions of the biota linked to the actions, concretions and formations of the land, the water and the air. Here Benjy might have had a slide, if he was still sitting in his booth.

A brilliant metaphor came out to attack the Gaia hypothesis. Imagine an airplane, it said. The airplane is packed with simple creatures, algae, worms, pea plants, horses. Even some highly intelligent creatures sit fastened in their seats. These pull the magazine out of the flap in front of them and ponder the cheerful people of far-off Burma. The more primitive biota simply sit, occupying their niches but not reading. They don't know how. But it doesn't matter. They fill their seats, and meanwhile, the airplane flies on. Mysterious mechanics have made it. It operates according to laws of physics and material science. Nothing the biota can do will influence the way it flies. Even if they vomit into those little bags, and make the cabin a reeking hell, this does not determine the airplane's flight. Your biota, it said to Gaia's face, are nothing more than these hapless passengers. They ride the earth through space, that's all.

The metaphor looked full in Gaia's eyes, then spat at her feet. It wheeled away, done with her, not even waiting for her retort.

Swarms of tiny invisible creatures came up and sucked the moisture from the spit. They carted away its enzymes, chopped its molecules into smaller strands. The airplane flew on. No one sat in its cockpit, yet the instruments lit up, red and green. Switches toggled, dials rotated. The biota in the seats grew restless. The flight was so long, they couldn't remember not flying. Sometime in their future, though, they would land at a gray, silent airport. No stewardess would wish them a pleasant journey. The door would open, and the biota would stream down the narrow passageway, clutching their bags. All the newsstands would be open but deserted, the magazine headlines blaring out, but no bored cashiers to take the money. Coffee bubbled at the coffee kiosk, steam rising behind the ranked paper cups and silver cream pitchers. But no one would charge them an astonishing price for it, to be paid out in foreign bills. The restroom hummed with a bluish light. When they opened the stall, plastic wrappings rotated around the toilet seat, offering up a sterile surface. When the biota sat down, and then stood up, the toilet flushed itself, waste draining away in the whirl of chlorinated water as if an invisible servant stood to hand. But there was no one. Some of the biota followed signs to the cabstand out front. They stood behind the sliding glass doors, looking out at the empty street. Slashed white lines painted on the pavement indicated it was safe to cross there, but they stayed where they were. No buses lumbered by. No men in uniform waved their arms, gesturing to go on or stop. One battered cab rolled up, the driver's seat unoccupied. The light on top indicated it was in service. Still the biota hesitated. They had no idea where it would take them.

A MIASMA

I'VE MADE SUCH A MESS of things. I left the latest clump of pages from Jonathan's binder outside when I ran in to get the phone. A woman asked for Jonathan, and I said he wasn't here. "Well, Barbara, I can talk to you, then," she said. "I'm not Barbara. This is Jenny," I said. "Jenny, please tell your father," she said, and reeled off complicated directions for getting to a golf outing. She hadn't seen him at it for many years. She was from the insurance agency, and should have known, I thought, his daughter's name, and that Jonathan was no longer a client. But she clung to her line that their clients were more like family friends, appreciating the personal service of the small agency, and she so looked forward to seeing Jonathan and Barbara and me and my brother as well at their annual event. It was almost an obligation, she implied. We had to show our appreciation for the agency's continued careful monitoring of our security and happiness.

"We'll be there," I said, to get her off the phone. I couldn't believe he'd ever golfed. He didn't like sports. Now he'll never golf, I thought. I sat by the phone, absorbed in wonder at the strange state he had blundered into. For me, he was dead and would never return, but for this persuasive Sherry at the insurance agency he was alive and hale, practicing his putting on a polished suburban lawn.

I didn't remember that I'd left the lecture notes outside until the next evening. Several pages had blown into the grass and gotten smeared with dew. I couldn't account for others that appeared to be missing. Jonathan may have lost these years ago, leaving them behind in a meeting room, on the lectern, or on top of a filing cabinet. So I had what looked to be only the very beginning of an explanation of the role of volcanoes in global cooling, once it was known that they were capable of releasing *a sunlight-veiling miasma of sulfuric acid.*

Despite these deplorable conditions, I am sure Jonathan would have said, let's go on from here. The partial nature of our evidence has not stopped us yet. Benjy, hop to it. The interglacial period that has seen the rise of human civilization is ending, and there can be little doubt that the great glaciers of the Ice Age will return. We have already endured this relatively benign interregnum for several thousand years longer than statistics would suggest is typical. Change may be gradual, or sudden, apocalyptic, and irreversible. Our own human endeavors may be adding to our danger, or may in the end alleviate the catastrophe. An Italian, he said, wrote a complete treatise on volcanoes, which he published under an assumed name, in the form of a letter between two young friends, most of it relating a dream that had visited Friend A in the night, followed by Friend B's interpretation.

"My bed erupted," wrote the first young man, "but rather than being harmed, I was carried on a mass of fire high into the atmosphere, and I was able to observe all the particulars of this domestic volcano." Here followed a disquisition on the composition of magma, couched as reverie because it contradicted the church's teaching that volcanoes seethed above pools of fat that combusted under the earth. Departing from this accepted science, Friend B described in his crude alchemical notation the chemical composition of unignited lava, as well as the shape of ash particles and the nature of the gases released.

This work circulated underground through the intelligentsia, until the church censorship bureau accosted its author. "It's only a dream I had," the author said. "I wrote it for the amusement of my friends. If it's traveled far, it's because many people were entertained by my silly story."

Then tell us another one, the clerical reviewer said. Tell us a light amusement with a pious point, so that we can learn from it enjoyably.

All of the succeeding pages are missing, as I've already noted. The students and I have little patience for chemistry, even of a primitive sort, and I'm sure they will forgive me for sticking in a story of my own here. As I've also noted previously, I type extremely quickly, and it will only take a few minutes for me to fill in a bit of narrative. A poor family rented out their soldier son's bedroom to a lodger, a single man, began the volcanologist. The daughter went out to work every day as a singing teacher, the father was ill, and the mother kept the house. Even with the lodger's money, they barely afforded the girl's nice clothes, which she required to keep her job. The mother wished the girl didn't have to walk to and fro across the town, because a series of gruesome stabbings made her worry. The victims were all young women, dragged into alleys, raped, and then horribly mutilated. The killer, the police thought, had to be a medical student, from the craft with which he disemboweled his victims.

The girl dismissed her mother's worries. "Those were all prostitutes," she said. "And far from here, or anywhere I have to go. Besides, I'm always home by shortly after dark."

The lodger kept to himself. His dark eyes and fine hands bespoke some mildness, yet he could be cold in the way he deflected his landlady's questions. He had paid them up front for a few weeks, and told them only that he needed quiet. He worked as a law clerk, he said, but didn't mention the name of the firm. Ink never stained his hands, yet at times the landlady noticed that he came home grimy, the knees of his pants caked in mud, one sleeve torn, rusty stains in the washbasin. The husband suggested they find a new lodger. This one wasn't quite steady. What did he do all day? Why did he come home so late? If only they didn't need his rent.

Excuse me, next slide please, Jonathan complained. Volcanoes, he said. Let's go on, he said, fixing the middle row with his acute gaze, glasses glinting. Sorry. Some extraneous material, perhaps inserted by my wife, who has decided tastes in literature and knows nothing about science. Benjy, slide. This grievous devastation, he said, is the ash-covered wreckage of the town of St. Pierre, where some 30,000 people died within the space of four minutes. Here began the modern study of volcanoes, which raised the possibility that two or three simultaneous eruptions could blacken the atmosphere to the extent that a shift towards planetary winter could not be avoided.

Next slide, please, I said. Benjy, please show a foggy street in which carriage wheels cut an eerie black geometry.

The boy in the slide booth doesn't respond to my commands, but it doesn't matter. The students move their pencils assiduously. We can still go on. Summer drew into fall and the lodger stayed on, said the volcanologist, putting the money in the landlady's hand every Wednesday. In all these months, they knew nothing more about him. He never mentioned his family, or spoke about a friend, or any acquaintance at his work. "Were you out last night with some of your pals?" the landlady asked him when he appeared at breakfast drawn, great purple circles under his eyes, scratches across his hand.

"Ha ha," he said. "My pals, yes." His neck too showed marks, disappearing into his collar. When he put a hand up to cover his cough, his sleeve fell back, revealing a row of red weals. The landlady was about to offer to clean them and put some ointment on them for him. When she looked up from his forearm, his eyes were on her, his face rigid with a kind of held-in contempt. She addressed a remark to her husband about the rain and cold, and took the dishes off the table.

The scientific community, Jonathan proceeded, speaking with a little more volume than was customary, has proved itself over and over again fickle, fallible, and blind to its own short-comings, as I may be myself. You want to know what happened? Slide please, Benjy, move on.

The church censor started back at the image of gray columns shrouded with dust, like rows of neglected ornaments in an abandoned room. Benjy has no picture for me, but for Jonathan he's put up what must be the next image in the lecture on the unprecedented global cooling that could be set off by two or three overlapping volcanic eruptions. The mathematics, Jonathan said, aids and supports Milankovitch's astronomical theory, which I'm afraid to say must now be dredged up from your notes, as it has come once again into favor.

This, Jonathan said, is, he said, but without more clarity, I can't complete what he would have indicated for a date or great-er geographical precision. The students hope this one will not appear on the exam. He wants to tell them about the sudden eruption of Mount Pelee, where the whole town below it was destroyed because the inhabitants had maintained that their safe-ty was in no way threatened. Newspaper reports described the town as having had no warning. Lava had poured out a notch in the top of the mountain and covered everything in a twin-kling, burning to a crisp even ships moored in the deep harbor. Yet letters and diaries discovered under the rubble described a series of escalating signs that the volcano was on the verge of violence. "We used to be able to see the mountain top from our back windows," wrote a wealthy lady to her sister in France. "But the black cloud of the last few days has blotted out everything." She described the vanished sound of the carriages in the street below: the ash lay almost a foot thick, and muffled the formerly ubiquitous clip-clop of the horses' hooves and the thin whine of the wheels rattling over the cobblestones. Eventually the persistent stench of sulfur led the inhabitants to only go out with their mouths covered with wet handkerchiefs. These shrouded pedestrians crept along the market street, barely visible in the murk, making no noise. Despite a rain of mud and tiny pellets of pumice stone, the lady's husband assured her that there was absolutely no danger.

In that case Jonathan won't mind if I go on with the story of the lodger: One evening came a terrible fog. In September, mist often wreathed the streets, hovering at ground level so that faces and hats floated above it, bodies below lost in white. This one lay denser than any seen before, an oily yellow pall shrouding the streets. The landlady peered from her open door, hoping to hear her daughter's footsteps. When the neighbor's door opened across the street, a little lighter rectangle pressed into the fog, but that was all. She called across to the neighbor. Their voices carried clearly, but neither woman could see the other. The husband lay panting in his chair. The fog had crept into the house. Its thick particles clogged his lungs. He groaned, and she ran to him. "Where's Anna?" he said. She was very late. The lodger had left before dinner and not been seen since.

I insist, said Jonathan. Jenny, really. I don't know where you've come across your information, but we were examining the eruption of Mount Pelee.

Just listen, I said. It's the same story, really.

The landlady would have gone out to meet the daughter with a lantern, but she was afraid to leave her husband. Every breath cost him, and the gap between each one stretched silently. The fog laid its fingers on her arm as she waited for the next creaking intake from the sick man in the chair. Then again came a stillness, broken after too long by a rattling, sputtering exhale. She held his hand. Every now and then he gave her hand a tiny squeeze, all he could do to encourage her. Everything would be fine, she told him voicelessly. Any moment they would hear the door, and the smack of Anna's hat hitting the table in the entryway. The lodger may have run into her at the end of the street, and both would come in together, laughing like young people.

Go on, said the church censor. What happened next?

Well the lodger, the volcanologist said, had a pair of very soft boots. He couldn't be heard when he came down the street. And the police had found a boot print at the scene of the latest killing, which they had copied to paper and carried around house to house, asking if anyone had its match. They knocked on the landlady's door. She answered reluctantly, not wanting to leave her husband. Just get all the shoes in the house, they said. It will only take a minute. They studied her husband's old shoes, though all he'd worn for months now was house slippers. Hers and her daughter's they disregarded. Anyone else at home, they asked? Just our lodger, she said. But he's not here right now. Are those his shoes in the hall, they asked? They were, but the soft boots were gone. She knew he must have worn them when he snuck out. They handled his other shoes, measuring them against the copy of the print from the scene of the crime. Similar size, they said. Very near. Perhaps we'll come back a little later to see him.

He's a very nice young man, she said. He'll be pleased to help you. He'll gladly show you his boots, which are nothing like the print you have there, she said. When they left, she ran into the lodger's bedroom, which he had given her permission to enter only once a week, to clean. In the dust by the washstand stood the faint impression of a boot. It's completely different, she told herself, though the distinct shape of the toe bore some resemblance to what the police had showed her. How could anyone be sure, she told herself. And what is a boot print, anyway? Everyone wears boots. There could be thousands of boots, exactly like those her lodger wore.

Jenny, Jonathan said. I don't know why you're being so insistent here. These are after all *my* notes. Let's go on with the eruption. A few weeks later, he said, the river tumbling down the mountain's slope into the harbor carried with it huge rafts of bird carcasses. The remains of small animals that had suffocated or burned came next, densely packed together so that the contingents of bodies moved like logs. Rotting animal flesh soon lined the harbor breakwater, the decomposing bodies seeming to twitch as the waves animated them. The town councilmen shouted to each other across the conference room, struggling to be heard over the noise as if from a cannon that now boomed from the mountain at continuous intervals. The councilmen concluded that there was no cause for worry. The volcano had never been known to erupt, and therefore they announced with certainty that it was not now about to do so. They ordered troops to patrol the road leading out of the town to stem an unruly tide of refugees. The soldiers turned back the wagons and laden mules, as well as the wily dockworkers on foot. There was absolutely no cause for alarm, they said, prodding with their bayonets.

And then, said the church censor. How was the husband's breathing? Did the daughter come home? Did the lodger come back? Did the fog cover everything, all night long? Did the land-lady notice blood dried to the washbowl?

Even more, said the volcanologist. The landlady poked in the lodger's dresser drawer, and found a leather sheath rolled up. It held a set of five thin surgical knives. Except that only four were in their slots. One was missing.

So then she was sure, said the church censor. She knew the lodger was the murderer, and she went out in the fog to find Anna.

No, no, she wasn't sure, said the volcanologist. Anyone could own a set of knives. Knives like that could be used for cutting up fowl. The lodger might have been a hunter. Maybe he enjoyed little trips into the country with dogs. That was why the knife was gone, the landlady thought. The lodger was a hunter, and not a failed medical student, out right now in the city streets, invisibly stalking beautiful long-haired girls like her Anna.

I don't believe it, said the church censor. She must have known who he was. He was the killer, right? The muddy trousers, the blood, the scratches, the soft boots. He must have been the murderer. And the landlady had seen him looking at Anna at mealtimes, measuring her under his lashes.

No, said the other. She couldn't believe that. The evidence fitted a different theory entirely. She needed the money the lodg-er gave her. Her husband was ill. She couldn't leave the house. And she had no reason to. She was sure that any minute now she would hear Anna rush in the door, the lodger with her.

Volcanoes, Jonathan said. Sulfuric acid. *A sunlight-veiling mias-ma.* That's what it says across the top of the page, even if the rest is blotted out. Clearly, Jenny, you can read that. The forces under the earth, he said, as they can't be seen, we feel free to ignore. We contradict the most flagrant of clues that they are soon to make themselves felt. The town suffered a plague of biting ants and centipedes that rushed down from the mountain top and overran a mill on the town's edges. The millworkers tried to stop them by overturning vats of lubricant oil on the horde, while the cooks and maids in the master's house smashed at them with their aprons and rolling pins. The insects were followed by snakes, including a particularly venomous genus of viper. These wriggled away from the now continuously belching mountaintop, biting any livestock they encountered in their escape. So not only did a torrent of writhing reptiles confront the residents of St. Pierre, but a slowly descending river of pig and cow corpses, puffed up and locked in rigor mortis, that the snakes had poisoned. The mayor nevertheless lowered the chain across the mouth of the harbor, refusing to let any ships leave that had not fully unloaded their supplies and reloaded with molasses, rum, and pepper. We are entirely safe, he announced at a ball held on the plaza that evening. The women brushed the falling ash off their gowns and ran off every few minutes to shake it out of their hair. In the ladies powder room, the wives and daughters stared at the women in the mirror, uniformly gray-haired and lined, themselves as they would be in twenty, forty, or sixty years. Yet all of them without exception died the next day as the lava overran the town, and so none of them had to endure their aging bodies, the dulled and weakened and wrinkled embodiment of the divine creatures waltzing at the harbor-side. No cause for alarm, read the last newspaper headline. Every one of them had agreed, the soldiers, the sailors, the scientists, the town councilors, and the women who hadn't dared to assert themselves. Even staring at the molten rock as it rushed towards them, they might have said to themselves and to each other, the mountain has never erupted and therefore it is not now erupting and cannot be doing so.

What a sweet, good nature you have, Jonathan said to me, that first evening when he took me to dinner at Puff's. When we stood to leave, he came around behind as if to pull out my chair. I had already stood, but he lunged at the chair back anyway, maneuvering the furniture aside with an appealing manly vigor. Then half behind me, half beside, he collapsed all his weight into me, his face in my hair. I stood stiffly, enduring this sudden revelation of his need. It's hard to know what I answered that with, even though only a few months passed between that night and our hurried, impulsive marriage.

In his after work hours, Jonathan sat in the midst of his scholarly apparatus, busily reading, scratching notes, or clacking the typewriter into life, small paragraphs from the sound of it, slow, untrained pecks. Somehow when I had lived alone, the desultory tasks that stretched through my solitude had seemed pleasant and endurable, but now I flipped through a magazine on jewelry design or watched "Chiller Theater" on Jonathan's wobbly television, feeling nothing but my separation from this man I had suddenly chosen to align myself with.

"Come to bed, Jonathan," I said to his bent head.

"You go on, sweetheart," he said. So tired from not having slept the night before and the night before that, I went upstairs. Hours later I awoke to find him lying next to me, the clock ticking, his breath coming in the soft, even furrows of unconsciousness.

NORTHWEST PASSAGE

LAST NIGHT I OPENED the study closet, a narrow affair with folding doors where Jonathan kept his office supplies and of course every other thing that made its way into his hands. His children's old artwork looked up at me, a fantastic tempera-paint dog's head with the body only faintly penciled in, atop a neat and elaborate maze. The first was the daughter's, the second the son's, unless I'm wrong. The children's tiny metal roller skates and broken tennis rackets mingled with Jonathan's own seldom-worn dress shoes, old briefcases and overnight bags, a roll of bandages, and the box of spare typewriter ribbons. I prized out what I wanted, a tightly lidded cardboard box in which he had not so long ago received a manuscript he was to review. He had saved it, along with other boxes of assorted shapes, in the dark below the bottom shelf. I shut the doors again and leaned against them while I pried the top off the box. The damp had softened the sides somewhat, and the cardboard left a dusty powder on my fingers, like the bloom on black grapes. But it wasn't too damaged for me to stow my manuscript in, once I completed my editing of his introductory course on the earth and its prehistory. When the top came free, a centipede ran out, skimming up the side, over my hand and falling to the floor as I shook it off me. I could have let it vanish into the baseboard, but I stamped on it, a good, quick grind with my slipper. Then it lay, not stuck to the sole but splayed on the hardwood like a model centipede, slightly elongated, legs on the left showing a little space between them and the central body core. It gazed up at me like a picture or an engraving of itself, life force gone due to my fierce thoughtlessness, but still here to remind me of what it had been.

We have five more minutes, Jonathan said. His students had already signaled the end of the period by slamming their notebooks shut, scuffing their feet, coughing rigorously, and upending from their slouches. Like performing seals cued to the chum bucket, they responded with delicate acrobatics to the slide of the minute hand towards half past the hour. And by contract they refused to understand or remember anything said in the final moments, even if they hadn't technically left their seats yet. Jonathan could slip anything he wanted into that last five minutes, take note, this will be on your quiz next week, he said, knowing the test itself would come as a complete surprise, and the questions appear intrusive, outrageous, the students would never expect themselves to be able to answer such queries. Imagine a future, he said, where the opposite of what we fear has happened. We've spent the semester wondering about the inevitable return of the ice. Now let's take a few minutes on this, our last day, to examine its opposite, the possibility of massive global warming. We have only at best competing theories for how the earth could have let herself be locked down in perpetual winter, and have spent little time forecasting an equally disastrous rise in overall temperature. Benjy, show us the Northwest Passage, he said. Yes, that's the one. Thank you.

The students squirm in their seats, a few girls in the front rows reluctantly but compliantly moving their pens over their notebooks, the rest holding their instruments slackly. It's too dark to see their watches, but the clock over Jonathan's head glows a skeleton of itself, phosphorescent dots ringing it, while two slim triangles mark the ghostly hands. As soon as the lights come on, it will flip back to a bureaucratic black and white, but now all eyes are on its strange, spare glimmer. Only two minutes left and he's still talking. The slide shows a painting of a wooden ship dwarfed by massive blue ice castles, anvils, Michelin men. Tiny figures in the foreground are caught in the instant of hauling black and brown packages, while nauseous arctic optical illusions bow the thin strip of sky above. This, he explains, is an artist's image of that unforgiving stretch of water, navigable for at most six weeks in high summer, at the top of the globe. Next slide, please, he says, but the students now slap their books shut. If their books were already shut, they open them so they can crack the air again with their stiff complaint. We're done. End of the hour. We refuse to listen or see.

It's only fair, isn't it, that they should turn away from what doesn't interest them, but Jonathan goes on with his second artist's version, a futuristic image of the same stretch of sea now only lightly plied with ice. The ice cutter, a steel and aluminum modern fantasy, high prow, ugly squat box mid deck, hoists and guns and antennae cluttering every other open space, pushes its way through a gray mush. The ice, such as it is, yields instantly, not to the superior technology of these twenty-first century sailors, but because it has no spirit. The tepid channel behind the ship bobs with plastic barrels, orange construction site netting, athletic shoes, telephone poles, sandwich bags, doll combs. Every kind of floating junk that populates the rest of the world also fills the ocean, forlorn, unnecessary, and insistently present beneath the teflon keel of the Intrepid VII. The ice had snapped the little wooden ship of the first slide between its jaws, the narrow leads of open water suddenly vanishing in front and behind. Though reinforced with teak, the strongest ship of its kind, enormously expensive, the pride of its nation, it was no match for the quick indifferent clasp of the sea ice. The ultramodern vessel, the one we can only imagine because the next century is almost twenty years away, is also the best of its kind, a special heated hull melting and radiating its way forward. But its effort is wasted. The water lies wanly blue between the feeble lanes of slush as the Intrepid VII noses forward. The crew unzip their foul weather gear and stand sweating in the few open spaces on deck, muscled out of the way by the enormous equipment. Clammy beads roll down the backs of their legs beneath the tight weave of their uniforms. They have nothing to do, and should revel in their leisure. With no ice to combat, they gaze at the floating junk, the surgical gloves, milk crates, and car tires slicked with shit. The flotsam curls aside as the ship bears down. The sailors and scientists would like to contest the ice, to fight and defeat it. But it reflects back to them not the harsh otherworldliness of sea ice but their own limp desires to do nothing at all, or nothing more than watch another video in the below-decks lounge.

When I first moved into Jonathan's house, unaltered since his first wife's time, I couldn't sleep, my first encounter with that terrible governor, insomnia. Though distressed, I felt in a way reassuringly adult, that mature people had this difficulty, lying awake in the dark next to a softly breathing foreign body. He had confessed to seizures of erotic fantasy about me that welled up as soon as we met, while for my part, his most appealing self was the sad man across the restaurant table, eyes draped in despair while the lower half of his face spun charming stories of late trains and lost boots. That man had vanished into a confident, routine-driven householder, his longing sopped by my presence near him. "All well, Jenny?" he asked, leaning over me as he exited his study. Over his ear I met the gaze of his typewriter, still warm from his exertions with it. Piles of paper occupied the desk on each side of the machine, the book he was writing, papers he'd graded, correspondence from colleagues, articles he reviewed anonymously as they were submitted to the mighty journal that published work from his sub-specialty. "Of course," I said. I didn't know what he did all day, or especially what he did in the evenings in that other room. What he wrote and marked up and muttered over, what he read and lectured upon, the earth and its prehistory, he saw no need to share with me. And I didn't ask. His actions had no overlap with my own, my precise and elegant typing during my work day, and later my poring over a magazine on jewelry design as if I might one day take up this art form. "Come to bed," I said, exhausted from not sleeping the night before. "You go on," he said, pulled back into his lair by a dense, gray monograph illustrated with a barely recognizable fragment of tibia. I watched him return his gaze to the papers in front of him, the hair on the top of his head looking sparser, and even that condemning me.

We have in the journals of Charles Murchison, sailor and botanist, he said, an account of an afternoon when his ship got stuck between two ice floes, and the men spent hours chopping a path to the free water they could see glinting through the alternating sun and fog. Only a few yards ahead of them, the ice parted around a clear lane of deep blue, but lodged as they were between two packets of ice, the current pulled them steadily back from it. Every inch of progress was reversed by the stronger hand of the arctic water. The men still on deck began shouting. On a neighboring ice floe appeared a mother polar bear and a beautiful little white cub. Murchison had forbidden them to shoot the bears, as they'd already found the meat inedible, and the liver, indeed, toxic. But he could hardly blame them for shooting just the little one. The animals must have come up out of the water, having swum near the ship to investigate. The mother shook droplets off her neck just like a hound dog. One of the men let off a perfect shot and took the cub right out from under her. They expected the adult to leap back into the sea at the crack of the rifle and leave them their prize. But she only looked around, knelt over the little thing, and moaned. As the current pulled them back, and their comrades doggedly hacked a passage free in front, still no one moved in relation to each other. The clear water came no nearer despite twenty men's efforts, and the patch of ice that held the bears remained stuck a little off to port. The mother prodded the unmoving little one with her nose and tapped it with her great front paw. Blood ran out of its neck and stained the channel pink. Captain Murchison berated them, though he knew the sailors had to have their sport. Locked here, perhaps desperately, and unable to steam out, he needed them to work willingly before they panicked. If the ice got too tight a hold, it would snap the keel, and they would have to abandon ship for the white wasteland. But the mother bear would not let up her mourning. Right next to them she howled and moaned, repeatedly rolling the baby's corpse and sniffing its open mouth. It was like having neighbors in the apartment just across the alley who fight by the open window every night, her calling him names until he slaps her, evening after evening because they just won't move away. So the sailors begged the captain to please let them shoot the mother bear. Put her out of her misery. We can't stand it, they said. She won't stop crying. She's so sad.

But it's your fault, he said. You have to stand it. This is what you did.

I lay the stack of Jonathan's almost completed lectures into the cardboard box, trying it out. It didn't fit. The sheets of paper, though all nominally the same size, had jostled each against each, the pages asserting themselves against their neighbors, so I couldn't rustle the pile into a neat edge. I held the paper upright over the table and tapped it down to align the bottom, but still when I set it into the container, some part stuck out, head or feet, and the body creased in the middle uncomfortably. Three, four times I worked the pile, holding it lightly between my fingers so the pages could slide into order. Though it looked like a dense, tight rectangle in my hands, it still resisted the dimensions of the manuscript box. The box must have been made to the specifications of another country's document system, where standard paper was not eight and a half by eleven but slightly smaller and measured out metrically or in an ancient idiosyncratic series of sizes, the quarto, the Becquerel, the barleycorn, the garn.

Jonathan leaned over me, putting his hands on my shoulders. I held still while his lips brushed my cheek and worked up through my hair. Though I could replay this scene, and countless others of our mild interactions, I couldn't redo them in a way that had me more than suffering his constant, grateful attention.

"Why don't you come to bed now?" I said.

Soon, he said, retreating. His tap-tapping at the typewriter accompanied my journey up the stairs. Through the floor came the shuffling of paper, the sigh, the creak of the chair as he shifted his weight. I fell asleep, and woke up a few hours later, alert to the ticking of the clock and Jonathan's perpetual, even exhalations.

THE MAMMOTH

THE CENSOR KNOCKED AGAIN on the volcanologist's door. Could you tell me just a little more, he said? I wondered if, at last, the landlady discovered anything.

The lodger snuck into the house, his soft boots crusted with dark material, his face scraped and bruised as if pushed against brick or cobblestone, his brown eyes beaming a happy exhaustion. The landlady called to him as he passed the door of the downstairs room her husband would shortly leave, though only in spirit. He didn't answer, but hurried on to his own room, where his splashing in the wash basin continued as a low under-current to the husband's drawn-out rasps. The possibility that volcanic eruptions had darkened the sky and masked the sunlight for just long enough to set off a swift decline into an ice age at-tracted sufficient support that it could not be entirely disproved, Jonathan said. The influence of the sun, he said, on the earth, and anything that comes between them, the difficulties, he said, orbital fluctuations, and the radiation, the heat, it's quite clear. Are you ready for your exam? Questions, he said? Yes, he said. Our maligned Milankovitch has come through almost unscathed. The evidence is so strong that other explanations must now be discarded or modified.

"Jenny," he said. "I have a proposition, or rather a proposal," using exactly that stiff, public voice. We were sitting next to each other on a bench behind the lecture hall, where we had gone to sit one other time. When I turned to face him, he was unable to go on. His mouth opened, and sweat beaded behind his glasses. Seeing he couldn't speak, I picked up his hand. I kissed the back of it, and he kissed mine. I understood him so well, I thought at that point. We didn't need to speak at all. I knew what he was asking me, and I had already decided to invite no one to the ceremony. I didn't need anyone else. I wanted to be alone with him, in what I imagined would be the beginning of an everlasting period of peace and stability.

When I first moved into Jonathan's house, his children's winter coats still hung on hooks in the hall. I supposed they needed them when they came back to visit, but only if they had ceased to grow when out of his sight. Relics of his travels crowned the fireplace mantel, while trophies of his abbreviated family life poked up everywhere, the listless ruffled curtains proclaiming a feminine taste, plastic zoo animals scattered underneath the couch where they had lain neglected for fifteen years.

"Sir, sir," the landlady called after him. He had given his name when he first moved in, but because of his shy mumble, she called him variously Mr. Tareyton, Mr. Tarringtown, Mr. Tessingdon, where all the previous lodgers, those who had skipped out on the rent after making such a fuss about meals, had gone by Bob, John, Eddy, and the one elderly one, Mr. Vane. In the instant of his creep past the open doorway, she had seen all she needed to see. But it was dark, she amended, and she instantly cast out the vision of his battered jaw and vulpine grin. He was a man, strong enough to go for the doctor, and that was all that mattered.

"I need your help," she said, knocking on his door. The water splashed in the basin, covering a squeak and mutter. "Sir, it's urgent," she said. She pushed the door open. The wood resisted, held back by a weight. He had pushed the bedside table against it. At two inches, the gap would not widen. But through the slit, she made out his shirtless torso bent over the basin. Lacerations crisscrossed his pale skin, old scars badly healed. Even the way he stooped communicated something slightly off to her, a childhood twistedness, an upsetting lack of symmetry.

But she needed him. "Sir, please," she called.

The lodger turned to her, his face a mix of fury, fear and delight. His teeth blasted a placating politeness, his eyes a triumphant evil, while the map of his face flickered, the muscles responding to his conflicting emotions. His wrists, hanging out of the pushed-up cuffs of his shirt, pooled pink into the basin.

"Yes?" he said.

"Excuse me," she said, backing away. She pushed the door shut and returned to her husband's side.

"Is Anna home? Is she safe?" the husband asked, his last words. He relapsed into shuddering, the breaths shaking his frame, his eyes cocked to the ceiling, unseeing.

"She's safe. Of course she is," said the widow. "I'm sure of it," she said, pressing his slack hand.

The evidence is so strong that we are forced to witness the shattering of our dearest wishes. Any questions? Benjy, pack up please. We won't need you next week for the exam. Please file the slides alphabetically by caption. You've done it before. I know you know the alphabet by now. Ha ha. Let's everyone thank Benjy for his service. Good boy. Thank you.

The students have already slipped from the auditorium. Those who remain, awkwardly pulling their coats around them, tap their fingers together to sign applause. Frankly, they haven't noticed the boy in the booth, and think they ought to applaud themselves for lasting out the semester.

Will we need blue books for the final, one asks?

Please be prepared, he answers. That's all he'll tell them.

But one more thought, he continues: in any case, no matter how your exams turn out, I hope you've gained something. This to their departing backs.

Oh yes, they mutter. They've gained a necessary credit in their distribution plan, so that they can go on and complete their degrees.

It's really a kind of thinking I want to get across, he explained to me. I was totally ignorant of his field, and tended to sink into my own concerns as soon as he delved into any kind of detail. I want them to be able to consider the world around them, he said.

Don't they do that already?

No, I don't think they do. They don't know how. They see what they want to see.

Really? I said, thinking of little things I had forgotten, to buy a card for a friend's birthday, to trim the cat's claws, so that the attentive face I held up to him masked thoughts trickling in all directions. He smiled, and who knows what was behind it, his display meeting mine, and both of us relieved, perhaps, that no significant transformation was required.

The next morning as I left for work, he leaned in to kiss me, and I swerved sideways. As we both righted ourselves, our cheeks passed by each other, only a few inches apart, so that my refused intimacy nevertheless took me through the field of his heat, the smell of his scalp and shaving cream. We both stood still, lingering on the outskirts of our disaster, the crater between us calmly filling with rainwater, garbage and dust.

"I'll see you this evening," he said.

"See you," I said.

Because I hadn't kissed him, he abruptly stuck his hand out and shook mine, as if I were a colleague, a realtor, an elderly cousin, or a reluctant recipient of a measly award. I wondered if this was good enough for him, if in fact he might like me better if I fell into some settled, lesser role. The entire geophysical story, he wrote, had been one of plasticity and change. But I doubt either one of us accepted that as fair. Whatever initial agreement there had been between us had rapidly mutated, as if without our volition. Surely we both hoped that it might swing back the other way. But what we ourselves might have done to make anything different, we seemed not to know.

When I turned my back on him to go out the door and walk to my bus stop, I still saw him, held in a lens in my mind, his face taut in an artificial cordiality. He looked almost as he had when I first met him, sweeping through the department office where I had been temporarily assigned, barely managing to check his fury and haste at the sight of the unknown woman at the desk. He had at that point too shaken my hand, crooking his Styrofoam cup into his elbow first, so that I had held my hand out, waiting, for a long time before he made good on the gesture. We seemed to have circled back to that initial wariness, two strangers politely touching. After months of living in his house, I knew him less well, saw only what I didn't understand about him. "I'm sorry," I should have said, and perhaps we could have started over. Instead we carefully hid our distress from each other, leaving that outer shell of geniality. The temperature and conditions on the inside were for both of us locked down, inaccessible.

When glacial time yawned open, his notes might here continue, it let out horrible beasts: the Irish elk, absurd antlers barring it from any forest, gigantic ground sloths and beavers, saber toothed cats, and worst of all, the mammoths. Siberian traders had been selling their tusks to the Chinese for a thousand years. They twisted off the ivory, leaving the rest to rot unexamined.

Many of the mammoths seemed to have died in mid-stride, sinking into muck that covered them over and extinguished them. Therefore they were usually found upright, deep under the ground as if they had been tunneling. The Chinese emperor entered them into his encyclopedia as a species of giant mole, eating their way through the darkness below the tundra. Once a surveyor reported finding one stuck in the bank of a river in flood. For eight days, he and his native crew had chugged their tiny steamboat upstream, though the current was barely discernible in places, and the whole course of the river had flattened out, subsuming all the surrounding plain. Ice, wood, mud, moss, tumbled by, until on the ninth day the water level dropped, and they tied up to wait for the men who were to guide them the rest of the way toward the gold mines. What looked like a rotting log dislodged and came floating at them. As the river twisted it, its skinny snout extended. The mammoth's trunk undulated in the water as if it were swimming, and its white eyes rose above the spray to glare at them. They almost capsized the boat, rushing first to one side to get away, then to the other to take a closer look. The thing came no nearer, though its heavy forelegs paddled darkly below the surface. Its brown body was long dead, and only half freed by the spring thaw. Icy mud still clutched its backside.

All the rest of the day they hacked at the bank with axes, and finally hauled it up to higher ground. As soon as the sun hit it, it began to rot. The fur steamed, and its fierce white eye turned in on itself. Its mouth lay open, the black tongue pooling into the mud. They took hold of it again to shift it further from the floodwaters. Its stomach snagged on a branch as they dragged it, and burst open. The mammoth had stood frozen and immobile beneath the mud for 40,000 years already. For those few moments, it had lived again, swimming so menacingly towards them that they almost overturned their boat. Now the ancient intestines rolled out of the slit, bearing a stench of death like a physical force. Startled by the slither of the innards around their ankles, the men jerked the corpse, and it snatched itself from their gloved hands. Gravity took it a few feet down the bank, and then the roiled water bore it under and away.

That afternoon I came home and twisted my key in the lock. The mechanism didn't give. It wasn't latched. He hadn't even shut the door tightly after me, after our last handshake, before the heart attack slumped him to the floor. I looked down at his body on the scuffed linoleum, the ruff of his thinned hair. Surely it's not over already, I said. Jonathan. Given that the nature of our world is one of fluctuation and change, it's not too late, I assured him. I put my hand on his neck. Cold rose up from his skin, unless the heat of my hand went down into it. He had already stiffened, so that he seemed to rebuff my probing touch. What a sweet, good nature you have, he might have said. He had continued to believe this about me, in spite of what I felt was accumulating evidence to the contrary. I'm sorry, I should have said. Let's start over.

I didn't say it, and at that point Jonathan too said nothing.

ACKNOWLEDGMENTS

SEVERAL KIND FRIENDS READ all or part of drafts of this book: Cooper Renner, David Isaacson, Gabe Blackwell, and Ammi Keller. Early portions of *Natural Wonders* were composed during a residency on Norton Island. I am grateful to the Eastern Frontier Educational Foundation for making that possible, and to John Beckman, John Rowell, Robin Martin, Ammi Keller, Josh Poteat and everyone else around the bonfire. Final chapters were written at the WormFarm Institute. Profound thanks to Jay Salinas and Donna Neuwirth for hosting me twice, and to Jeff Spoon, Betsy Arant, and everyone else involved in that lovely venture in the Driftless. Thank you to my employer, Edgewood College, for supporting my work, particularly to Dean Pribbenow and Kris Mickelson, who helped me find time to write. Thank you, Isabel. Thank you, Abner.

Chapter ten, "Lake Vostok" appeared in *Black Warrior Review*. The chapters "Ice Ages," "Small, Bitter Victory," "Astronomical Theory," "The Modern," and "Gaia" appeared in *Western Humanities Review*.